Clements R. Markham

A Memoir of the Lady Ana de Osorio

countess of Chinchon and vice-queen of Peru - A. D. 1629-39 - with a plea

for the correct spelling of the Chinchona genus

Clements R. Markham

A Memoir of the Lady Ana de Osorio
countess of Chinchon and vice-queen of Peru - A. D. 1629-39 - with a plea for the correct spelling of the Chinchona genus

ISBN/EAN: 9783337383138

Printed in Europe, USA, Canada, Australia, Japan

Cover: Foto ©Andreas Hilbeck / pixelio.de

More available books at **www.hansebooks.com**

A MEMOIR

OF THE

LADY ANA DE OSORIO

COUNTESS OF CHINCHON

AND

VICE-QUEEN OF PERU

(A.D. 1629–39)

WITH A

Plea for the Correct Spelling of the Chinchona Genus

CLEMENTS R. MARKHAM, C.B., F.R.S.

Commendador da Real Ordem de Christo. Socius Academiæ Cæsareæ Naturæ Curiosorum,
Cognomen CHINCHON

LONDON
TRÜBNER & CO., LUDGATE HILL
1874

PREFACE.

—*o*—

FIFTEEN years ago the Chinchona trees, which yield quinine and other febrifuge alkaloids, were only found wild in the forests on the slopes of the cordilleras of the Andes. Now they are carefully cultivated in British India and Ceylon, in Java and Jamaica. The beautiful trees, with their glossy leaves and fragrant racemes of flowers, cover the sides of the Dodabetta peak, the slopes · overhanging Wynaad, and the hills at Rungbi in Sikkim. They yield thousands of pounds of bark, which will soon be supplied, in the form of a cheap medicine, to the millions of fever patients of India, while they also, by the sale of the higher-priced barks in the London market, give a remunerative return to the Government. They form one of the most useful products of British India, as of Ceylon and Java; and their name is not now merely a botanical term, but one

b

which is in constant use by the administrator, the chemist, the physician, the planter, and the merchant, and which should retain a grateful place in the memories of thousands whose restoration to health is due to the use of quinine.

To all such, to all who are interested in Chinchona cultivation, the origin of the name cannot fail to be a matter of some interest; and when it is known that the trees received it in honour of a gracious lady who first made their healing virtues known in Europe, a desire to learn something of her history is surely natural.

It was with such feelings that, when an opportunity offered, the writer of the following short and imperfect Memoir devoted such time as was at his disposal, during the intervals snatched from more absorbing work, to the collection of all the information that he could find respecting the Countess of Chinchon, and to visits to the places of her residence in Spain. His time was unfortunately short, and it was mainly taken up in the preparation of the official reports mentioned in the footnote.* The Memoir is the result of a

* 1. *Report on the Irrigation of Eastern Spain, containing a Historical Summary of Moorish works, and details of the systems in the*

few intervals of leisure. It is an imperfect but a zealous attempt to revive the memory of the Countess of Chinchon, who was truly one of the greatest benefactors of the human race.

In the following pages will be found a history of the Osorios, the paternal ancestors of the Countess, and of the family of her husband; accounts of the government of Peru under the viceroyalty of the Count of Chinchon;* of the famous cure of the Countess, and of her introduction into Europe of the use of fever-dispelling bark; and a detailed

---

valleys of Murcia, Orihuela, Crevillente, Elche, Alicante, Novelda, Játiva, Gandia, the Xucar, Valencia, Castellon, Vinaroz, and Beni-carlo; with maps and plans. By Clements R. Markham, F.S.A.

2. *Report on the Specimens of Chinchona in the Herbaria at Madrid, including the Collections of Ruiz, Pavon, and Tafalla.* By Clements R. Markham, F.S.A.

3. *The Chinchona Species of New Granada, printed for the first time from manuscripts at Madrid, with a Memoir of Don José Celestino Mutis.* By Clements R. Markham, F.S.A.

* I have collected the few particulars respecting the history of the Count's viceroyalty from various sources. But it was disappointing to find so little in the famous metrical history of the conquest of Peru and of the Viceroys by Dr Pedro de Peralta y Barnuevo. (*Lima Fundada, Poema Heroica.* Lima, 1732.) The part referring to the Count of Chinchon is included in nine stanzas, two devoted to the celebration of that nobleman's high qualities, and the rest to a record of some foolish miracles during the earthquake at Lima on 17th November 1630. Dr Peralta describes the Count as a compound of Cato and Mecænas, as able, benevolent, and just. (*Lima Fundada*, Pte. II. canto vi. 10 to 18.)

description of the town of Chinchon, its castle, church, houses, and neighbourhood. Finally, there is a plea for the correct spelling of the Chinchona genus, on the ground that thus only can that honour which it so fully merits be done to the memory of the Countess. The word is now in common use; it is not merely a scientific term; and the question whether it shall be spelt so as to recall the memory of the Countess, or so that her name shall be disguised and mutilated, is a question which concerns all who, from whatever cause, take an interest in the history, in the cultivation, in the use, or in the commerce of Chinchona bark.

TABLE OF CONTENTS.

———o———

Contents.

LIST OF ILLUSTRATIONS.

Arms of Osorio,

MARQUISES OF ASTORGA.

Or two wolves passant gules: on a base argent three lines of waves paly azure: the whole surrounded by eight shields of the arms of Henriquez, on an orle azure.

THE LADY ANA DE OSORIO,

COUNTESS OF CHINCHON.

I.

Che Osorios.

HE noble lady who first brought the fever-
dispelling bark - powder from Peru to
Europe, and whose name would be
justly immortalised in the *genus* which yields the
bark, if, by an unfortunate misapprehension, it had
not been so frequently misspelt, was a daughter of
the ancient Spanish family of Osorio.

This family is of extreme antiquity. Indeed, we
are told by the painstaking old Father Morote that
their ancestor was a son of Nebuchadnezzar, who
was sent by his father with a colony of Jews to
Spain.*

The cradle of the Osorios was in Galicia ; and in

---

* *Antiguedad y blasones de la ciudad de Lorca*, por Padre Morote
(Lorca, 1740), Pte. II. lib. i. cap. 19, p. 230.

A

reality they appear in the very dawn of the struggle between the little band of hunted Goths, in the mountain fastnesses of Galicia and the Asturias, and the civilised power of Mussulman Spain. Surely, at its commencement, no struggle ever appeared more unequal.

Ramiro I. ascended the precarious throne of the Christian kingdom of Galicia in 843 A.D., when the great and enlightened Khalífah Abdu-'r-Rahmân II. was reigning over the rest of Spain. The Khalífah proclaimed the usual holy war, and sent an army over the frontier, while the hunted Christians strained every nerve to assemble a sufficient force to resist the invasion. In the first encounter, near Albeyda, Ramiro was routed, and his army was only saved by the approach of night. But the Apostle St James appeared to him in a vision, and told him that if he fought boldly on the following day, victory was certain. St James, mounted on a white horse, led the Spaniards into battle; the Moors were defeated, and 60,000 were killed in the pursuit. Thenceforward *Santiago* became the battle-cry of Spain. In this battle of Clavijo, which took place in 844 A.D., a knight named Osorio fought side by side with St James, and his descendants are, in consequence, hereditary Canons of Leon, with an appropriate stall in the Cathedral.*   •

Don Alvaro Nuñez Osorio, a descendant of this famous knight, was the favourite of King Alonzo XII., who created him Count of Trastamara, and this creation is the most ancient instance of such a ceremony on record in Spain. The King, being seated in a chair of state, was presented with a cup of wine containing three sops. He then solemnly bade Don Alvaro take one, and Alvaro bade the King, in the same phrase. " *Tomad Conde*" and " *Tomad Rey*" were the words. After this mutual salutation, they ate the sops together, and the knights who stood by hailed Alvaro by acclamation with the name of *Conde.*† Then a banner and a caldron ("*peñon y caldera*"),‡ and possessions fit for

---

* *Mariana, Hist. de España* (ed. Madrid, 1794), vol. ii. p. 310; *Lopez de Haro*, vol. i. p. 293. On 1st February 1602, King Felipe III. and Pedro Alvarez Osorio, eighth Marquis of Astorga, as hereditary Canons of Leon, both sat in their stalls in the quire of the Cathedral, and received their fees for attendance.

† *Mariana*, lib. xv. cap. 20; tom. iv. p. 110 (Span. ed. Madrid, 1794); *Selden's Titles of Honour*, Part ii. cap. 4, p. 473.

‡ The banner was a token of power, given to a Count to lead in the field, and the caldron of his greatness in housekeeping, and ability to maintain those whom he should lead. These insignia entitled him to prefix the title of *Don* to his name, which was only used, in early times, by the King, the Infantes, Prelates, and Ricos-hombres, in-

a Conde, were given him by charter. The ceremony took place at Seville, in the year 1328.*

The title of Trastamara seems to have passed
away from the Osorios, for a time, after the death
of the first Count. Enrique II. enjoyed it before
he became King, and afterwards it was granted to
the Castro family.

Pedro Alvarez Osorio was Adelantado of Leon
in 1349, during the reign of Pedro el Cruel, who
caused him to be assassinated at Villanubla, while
sitting at dinner with the Master of Calatrava, for
having remonstrated against the tyrant's atrocities.
The Adelantado married Maria Fernandez de
Villalobos, daughter of Doña Inez de la Cerda,
and granddaughter of Alonzo de la Cerda, who was
a son of Fernando, the Infante of La Cerda, and
eldest son of King Alonzo the Wise, by Blanche
of France (daughter of St Louis). The Infantes
of La Cerda were the discarded, but rightful heirs
to the throne of Castille.

---

cluding all the Condes. *Rico-hombre* signified, in early times, what
Grande does now—a man rich in honour and nobility, not in money.
The latter quality would be indicated as *Hombre-rico.*—*Salazar de
Mendoza.* The caldron (*caldera*) was frequently used in the armorial
bearings of Spanish noblemen.

* *Cronica del Rey Don Alonso el ultimo*, cap. 64.

The Adelantado was buried in the Church of San Domingo at Benavente, ten leagues from Astorga, by the side of his father.

Alvaro Perez Osorio, Count of Villalobos in right of his mother, was the Adelantado's son. When John of Gaunt, Duke of Lancaster, claiming the throne of Castille by right of his wife, the daughter of Pedro el Cruel, landed at Coruña with a small force of Englishmēn in 1384, his advance was opposed by the Count of Villalobos. The Count, assembling all his friends and vassals, attacked and routed the English, who retreated to Valderas. The inhabitants of that village left their cellar doors open, and put a quantity of salt into the wine. The more the English fugitives drank, the more thirsty they got, until they became insensible, and were easily killed. John of Gaunt's invasion ended in his expenses being paid, and his daughter Catharine being married to the heir of Castille. The Count was afterwards Captain-General on the Moorish frontier, where he maintained 400 cavalry at his own charges. Once, while in this command, the King came to visit him, and Osorio invited his Majesty to dine in his house. The King readily consented, and the meal being served up on wooden dishes, he inquired why silver was not used. ' Osorio gave as a reason that he generally had to eat standing, with the dish in his hand. The King was pleased with the answer, and presented Osorio with a silver plate weighing 300 marks.* The original grant of this dish is preserved in the archives of Astorga. Soon afterwards the King again visited his Captain-General, and being once more served on a wooden trencher, he inquired where the silver dish was. Osorio replied that he would show his Majesty after dinner, and taking him to a window, he pointed to a troop of cavalry, which he had equipped for the cost of the silver dish. He died in 1396, and was also buried at Benavente.

His son, Juan Alvarez Osorio, Count of Villalobos, was Chamberlain to Enrique III. and his wife Catharine of Lancaster in 1406. He afterwards served with great distinction in the Moorish wars, under Juan II., and died in 1417. He was buried with his ancestors in the Church of San Domingo at Benavente.

Pedro Alvarez Osorio, his son, succeeded him as

---

* *Nobiliario genealogico de los titulos de España*, por Alonzo Lopez de Haro (Madrid, 1722), vol. i. p. 275.

Count of Villalobos. He did good service to Juan
II. at the battle of Olmedo in 1445, when the Aragonese were defeated; in reward for which the
King created him Count of T,rastamara, a title
which had once been held by one of his ancestors,
and which had now become vacant through the
death of Don F. de Castro, Duke of Arjona. (See
page 4.) The grant is dated from Valdeiglesias, on
February the 4th, 1445. Afterwards the Count was
incessantly mixed up in the intrigues of the court
of Juan II., and in 1461 he appears to have been
poisoned. He was buried in a Dominican convent
which he had built near Valderas.

Alvaro Perez Osorio, his son, the second Count
of Trastamara, is said to have been very handsome
and of noble bearing. As many as 200 gentlemen
were constantly in attendance on his person, with
arms and horses; and he was looked upon, in the
court of King Enrique IV., as the mirror of knight-
hood and courtesy. When the Infante Alonzo re-
belled against the King his brother, the Count of
Trastamara brought a large force to the loyal side,
and was so rapid in his attacks, that the enemy
nicknamed him Alvaro Madrugo (*Alvaro the early
riser*). At last the rebels resolved to try if an in-

cursion into his own land would not draw off his troops from the King's service. But, without leaving the royal camp, the Count sent such help to his brothers Diego and Luis as enabled them to drive back the invaders with great loss.

At the successful conclusion of this war, King Enrique offered him his choice of a title from the towns of Coruña, Lugo, or Astorga, with the rank either of a Duke or Marquis. The Count kissed his sovereign's hand, and modestly selected the title of Marquis of Astorga. This was in July 1465, and the very curious patent of Marquis is given in full by Lopez de Haro.*

In 1466, the first Marquis of Astorga was engaged in suppressing the rebellions of the brotherhoods (*Hermandades*), the lower orders of Galicia and the Asturias, who rose against the intolerable oppressions of the nobles.

The first Marquis of Astorga married Leonora, daughter of Don Fadrigue Henriquez, Admiral of Castille, when he adopted an orle of the Henriquez arms as an addition to his own coat. This lady was

---

* *Nobiliario*, vol. i. p. 281 ; also inserted, in full, in *Selden's Titles of Honour*, p. 466.

a sister of the Queen of Aragon, mother of King Fernando the Catholic. The Marquis died in 1471, and was buried with his wife in the Cathedral of Astorga.

Pedro Alvarez Osorio, the second Marquis, succeeded to his title and estates just when the war of succession broke out between the King of Portugal and Isabella the Catholic. Although he was only fourteen years old, the young Marquis assembled his vassals, and joined Isabella's camp at Toro with 2000 men, in July 1475. In the subsequent battle, this gallant boy was the first to lead his men against the enemy, and, with the Duke of Alva, turned their flank, and completed their disorder. He afterwards served with distinction at the siege of Granada, and was present at the capitulation of the Moorish King on the 30th of November 1491. He died in August 1505, and was buried with his parents in the Cathedral of Astorga.

At the courts of Juan II., and of his children, Enrique IV. and Isabella the Catholic (A.D. 1407 to 1504), most of the nobles cultivated the art of poetry, the most eminent being the Marquis of Santillana. Among the minor poets was the second Marquis of Astorga, one of whose love-songs is

B

given in the *Cancionero General.** This song is
written in the old Spanish measure and metre, in
coplas or stanzas, the metre being the same as that
adopted in the exquisitely beautiful contempora-
neous poem of Jorge de Manrique, which has been
translated by Longfellow. The song of the Marquis
of Astorga is addressed to the lady of his love,†
and is as follows (*Can. Gen.* fol. 154, Anvers,
1573):—

---

* The "*Cancionero General*," or *General Collection of Poetry*, was
first printed at Valencia in 1511, by Fernando del Castillo. It contains poems attributed to more than a hundred different persons. In
1514, a new edition appeared, and six others had followed, at Toledo
and Seville, before 1540. In 1557 and 1573 two enlarged editions
appeared at Antwerp. The work contains the body of poetry most in
favour at court, and in the more refined society of Spain, during the
fifteenth century—many works of the most notable Troubadours of
Spain, in devotion, morality, love, jests, ballads, devices, mottoes, and
glosses. The principal authors are the Marquis of Santillana, Juan
de Mena, the Manriques, the Viscount of Altamira, Lopez de Haro,
the Marquis of Astorga, Luis de Vivero, Hernan Mexia, &c. &c.—
Ticknor's Spanish Literature, vol. i. p. 395.

† It is to be hoped that the lady was his young wife, Beatriz de
Quiñones, daughter of the Count of Luna, a notable warrior in the
Moorish wars, by his wife Juana de Henriquez.

COPLAS

DEL MARQUES DE ASTORGA.

A su amiga.

—o—

I.

Esperanza mia, por quien
Padece mi corazon
Dolorido.
Ya, Señora, ten por bien
De me dar el galardon
Que te pido.

II.

Y pues punto d'alegria
No tengo ; si tu mi dexas
Muerto se.
Vida de la vida mia,
A quien contare mis quexas
Si a ti no ¿

III.

Aquel Dios d'amor tan grande,
Que consuela a los vencidos
Amadores ;
De mando soluto mande
Que hieran en tus oidos
Mis clamores.

IV.

Y la justa piedad
Que a persona tan hermosa
Pertenece,
Incline tu voluntad
A mi vida dolorosa
Que padece.

V.

Y aquel tanto dessear
Que haze ser porfiado
Al amante,
Que no le dexa mudar,
Mas quanto mas penado
Mas constante ;

VI.

Y lo que haze andar mustias
A las amantes mugeres
Medio muertas,
Te haga que mis angustias
En señaladas plazeres
Me conviertas.

VII.

Y aquel gran dolor que suele
Inclinar las mas essentas
A mesura,
Te duela, que si te duele,
No puede ser que no sientas
Mi tristura.

VIII.

Do quiça podra nacer,
Que con la penada vida
Que viviesses,
Viendo mi gran padecer,
Tu misma de ti vencida,
Te venciesses.

IX.

Torre de omenage fuerte,
Fortaleza que tan bella
Me parece,
Congoxa d'amor despierte
Tu corazon, que sin ella
Se adormece.

X.

Arco de flechas raviosas,
Que mi salud desesperas,
Sabe cierto,
Que si todas esas cosas
No te hazen que me queras,
Yo soy muerto.

XI.

Escucha los mensageros,
Que llenan nuevas estrañas
Que te harten,
Mis sospiros verdaderos,
Que me arrancan las entrañas
Quando parten.

XII.

Y sienten mi gran passion,
Con que yo te los embio,
Pacediente;
Y sienta tu corazon
La grave pena que el mio
Por ti siente.

XIII.

Que sino te veo, muero,
Con la soledad que acusa
Mi venida;
Y en viendo te desespero,
En pensar que no se escusa
La partida.

XIV.

Entonces siento un plazer,
Rebuelto con un dolor
Que me engaña.
Y quando quiero escoger
Lo que pienso que es mejor,
Mas me daña.

XV.

Y soy tal como doliente ·
A quien la dolencia estrecha
Se le alarga.
Que lo malo les plaziente
Y lo que mas le aprovecha
Mas le amarga.

XVI.

Es mi vida una morada
Donde vienen los tormentos,
Cuya puerta
A mis bienes es cerrada,
A mis tristes pensamientos
Muy abierta.

XVII.

Mas con la sobra del miedo
La mi lengua tornaria
Medio muda.
No hare poco si puedo
Recontar la pena mia
Que es sin duda.

XVIII.

Ante ti el seso mio
Siente tantos alboroços
De turbado,
Como quando va el Indio
Por el monte de Toroços
Al mercado.

XIX.

Que mil años estuviese
Mirando tu gentileza
Partiria,
Al tiempo que me partiesse
Con essa misma tristeza
Quedaria.

XX.

Tal padezco yo en pensar
Atajar por tal camino
Mis passiones.
Como quien piensa matar
Con un gran monton de lino
Los tizones.

XXI.

Aquel gran fuego de amar
Que mis entrañas atiza
Tal me tiene.
Ni me dexa de quemar
Ni me convierte en ceniza
Porque pene.

XXII.

Mas fuego casi semprende ·
Quien pondra sufrir, señora,
Vida mia.
Que su flama que me enciende
Dos tanto me quema agora
Que solia.

XXIII.

Y aqueste papel morado
De la tinta con que escrivo
El mal que tengo,
Ya deve enojado
Pues que hare yo cativo
Que sostengo.

XXIV.

Muchas mas tribulaciones
Que es impossible contar
Pues tu cata,
Remedio de mis passiones
Como me puedas sanar
Bien o mata.

XXV.

Que mi lengua te alabe
En aquestos mis renglones
Ya concluyo,
Pues que todo el mundo sabe
Que tengo cien mil razones
De ser tuyo.

XXVI.

Y esta mi grossera mano
No piensa poder loarte,
Ni se atreve,
Porque mi seso villano
No puede saber mirar te
Quando deve.

XXVII.

Assi los tus loores
Recontar en ningun modo
Yo no quiero,
Ni grave de mis dolores
Pues que sabe el mundo todo
De que muero.

XXVIII.

Que mi sentido en lo uno
He miedo que se turbasse
Con amor,
Quien no seria importuno
Si todo escrevir pensasse
Su dolor.

CABO.

Dime para quando guardas
Desta mi pena tan fuerte
De librarme,
Cata que si mucho tardas
Poco tardara la muerte
De llevarme.

Y todo sara dezir
Assi goze que de veras
He pesar,
O que buen arrepentir,
O que donosas maneras
De matar.

It was in the time of the second Marquis that the present Cathedral at Astorga was built, having been commenced in the year 1471, on the site of a more ancient edifice. Mr Street gives the following account of Astorga Cathedral :—" It is of the latest Gothic style, much of the detail being renaissance in character. The windows are filled with a good deal of fine early stained glass; but beyond a certain stateliness of height and colour, there is but little to detain or interest an architect. But stateliness and good effects of light and shade are so very rare in modern works, that we can ill afford to regard a building which shows them as being devoid of merit or interest." *

The castle or palace of the Osorios was somewhat older, and the streets of Astorga were full of the houses of gentlemen or hidalgos, some of them cadets of the family, all followers of the great Marquis at court and in the field. Poetry, architecture, and other arts of peace were studied by the Osorios of Astorga in the fifteenth century; and the knights who had fought in many a stricken field against the infidels of Granada were ardent cultivators of literature and the fine arts.

---

* *Gothic Architecture in Spain*, chap. vi. p. 130.

The second Marquis of Astorga married a young lady whose father had fought side by side with him in the war of Granada. This was Doña Beatriz de Quiñones, daughter of Diego Hernandez de Quiñones, Count of Luna, by his wife, Juana Henriquez, daughter of the first Count of Alba de Liste. His children were—

1. Alvaro Perez, the third Marquis.

2. Diego, Lord of Losada, and Commander of Ocaña.

3. Teresa, married to Rodrigo de Castro Osorio, Count of Lemos. They had a daughter and heiress named Beatriz, who succeeded as Countess of Lemos in her own right, and married twice—first, to a Portuguese Prince, son of the Duke of Braganza, and secondly to Don Alvaro Osorio, a grandson of the first Count of Trastamara. Her daughter Maria, by the second marriage, was wife of Don Juan Alvarez Osorio, a younger son of the third Marquis of Astorga.

Alvaro Perez Osorio, the third Marquis, went with King Fernando to receive Juana and her husband, Felipe, when they landed in Galicia, and he afterwards entertained Fernando for three days at Astorga. He received the Order of the Golden

Fleece from Carlos I., when that monarch held the Cortes at Coruña, and embarked for Germany in May 1520, leaving Cardinal Adrian as 'Regent of Spain. The Marquis returned to Astorga; but he had not been there long before the news reached him of the insurrection of the *Comunidades* in Castille. He assembled all his people, joined the Cardinal, and soon afterwards captured Tordesillas, thus securing the person of the insane Queen Juana, who had previously been in the hands of the *Comuneros.* In January 1523, while he was with the Court at Valladolid, the Marquis of Astorga died, and was buried in the cathedral of his native city, with his fathers.

Pedro Alvarez Osorio, the fourth Marquis, was in Rome when it was sacked by Bourbon's army. Pope Clement took refuge in the Castle of St Angelo; and when the enemy attempted to force an entrance, the Marquis of Astorga stood at the door with his drawn sword, and made them so eloquent a speech that they gave up their intention. The grateful Pope gave him a piece of the winding-sheet of Lazarus, and an emerald salt-cellar, which was entailed as an heirloom. The Marquis accompanied Carlos I. on his expedition to Tunis, attended by many relations and vassals; and he also served with

C

the Emperor in Flanders and Germany. He was famous for his great wealth, and for the costly magnificence of his entertainments. He died in Valladolid in 1560, having had by his wife, Maria Pimentel, daughter of the Count of Benavente, three sons :—

1. Alvaro Perez Osorio, fifth Marquis of Astorga, who was a very religious man, and had a private musical chapel in his house. He died at Astorga in 1567, leaving, by his wife, Beatriz, a daughter of the Duke of Alva, a son—Antonio Pedro Alvarez Osorio, sixth Marquis of Astorga, who was very fond of horse-exercise, but he died at the early age of eighteen, on February 12th, 1579, and was buried in the Cathedral of Astorga.

2. Alonzo Perez Osorio, seventh Marquis of Astorga, was a Knight of Alcantara. He accompanied Felipe to England when he married Queen Mary, and continued in his service afterwards, dying at Valladolid on Christmas Day 1592.

3. Pedro Alvarez Osorio, married Doña Constanza de Castro Osorio, and had a son, Pedro Alvarez, the eighth Marquis.

Pedro Alvarez Osorio, eighth Marquis of Astorga, was of extremely blue blood—"*sangre muy*

azul;" for no less than two of his grandfathers
and one of his grandmothers were Osorios. He
was brought up first as a page of honour to Felipe
II.'s last queen, Anne of Austria, and afterwards
with his uncle, the seventh Marquis. He was a
nobleman of cultivated taste and considerable ability,
and was very fond of architecture. This Marquis
was a Knight of the Habit of Calatrava. He married Doña Blanca Manrique y Aragon, daughter of
Don Luis Fernandez Manrique, Marquis of Aguilar,
by his wife, Ana de Mendoza y Aragon. The eighth
Marquis of Astorga died, at the age of forty-nine, in
the city of Astorga, on the 28th of January 1613,
and his wife, Doña Blanca, followed him on March
25th, 1619. She died at Valderas. They were
buried together, in the Chapel of the Osorios, in
Astorga Cathedral. They left three children, one
son and two daughters:—

1. Alvaro Perez Osorio, ninth Marquis of Astorga,
succeeded his father when only thirteen years of
age. He was born on February 28th, 1600. Lopez
de Haro tells us that he was not yet married when
he wrote concerning the Osorios in 1620; but in
1769 his descendant was the heiress Doña Nicolasa
de Osorio, Marchioness of Astorga, Countess of

Trastamara, &c.˙ The present Marquis of Astorga has a large house at Madrid. The Marquises are hereditary Canons of Leon, because their ancestor, in A.D. 846, fought side by side with Santiago at Clavijo.

2. Constanza, married to the Marquis of San Roman.

3. ANA, the future COUNTESS OF CHINCHON, and Vice-Queen of Peru.*

---

* *Nobiliario de los Reynos y Señorios de España,* por Don Francisco Piferrer (Madrid, 1858). Argote de Molina.

II.

Laby Ana be Osorio.

HE Lady Ana de Osorio, youngest daughter of the eighth Marquis of Astorga, was born in the year 1599, in her father's palace at Astorga, the ruins of which yet remain. Ford says, " A portion of the fine library fortunately escaped Soult's camp-fires, and now belongs to the Advocates at Edinburgh." Junot destroyed the old palace in April 1810, and only two towers, with some armorial shields, remain.

The Lady Ana's father died in his palace at Astorga on the 28th of January 1613, aged forty-nine, and her mother died at Valderas on March 25th, 1619. They are both buried in the family chapel in the Cathedral of Astorga.

Two years after her father's death, the youthful Lady Ana, then only sixteen years old, was taken from her home amidst the pleasant highlands of

OSORIO,

MARQUISES OF ASTORGA: CREATED 1465 A.D.

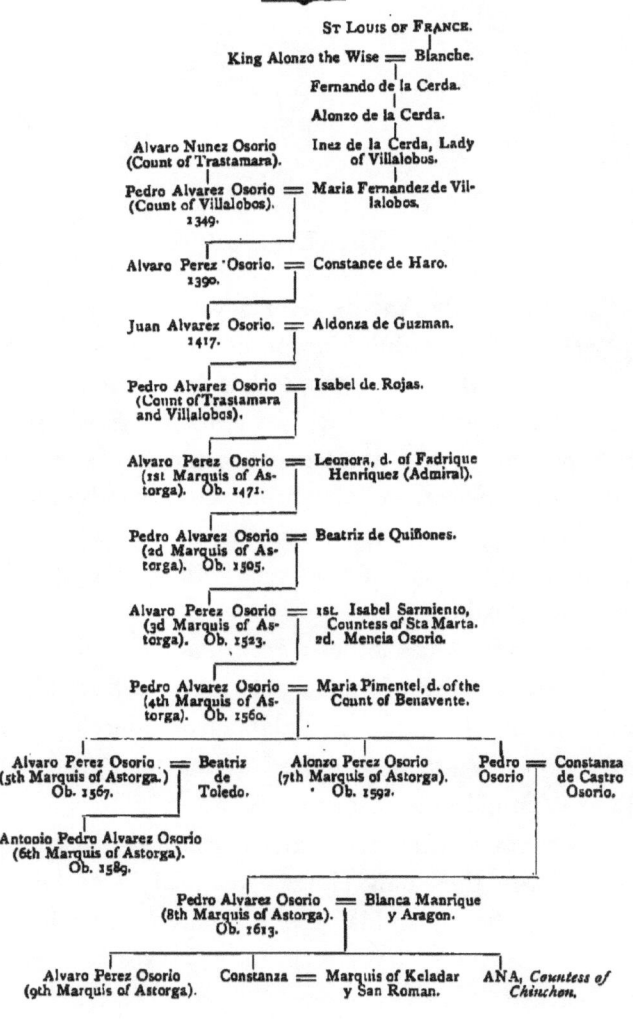

ST LOUIS OF FRANCE.

King Alonzo the Wise == Blanche.

Fernando de la Cerda.

Alonzo de la Cerda.

Alvaro Nunez Osorio   Inez de la Cerda, Lady
(Count of Trastamara).   of Villalobos.

Pedro Alvarez Osorio == Maria Fernandez de Vil-
(Count of Villalobos).   lalobos.
1349.

Alvaro Perez Osorio. == Constance de Haro.
1390.

Juan Alvarez Osorio. == Aldonza de Guzman.
1417.

Pedro Alvarez Osorio == Isabel de Rojas.
(Count of Trastamara
and Villalobos).

Alvaro Perez Osorio == Leonora, d. of Fadrique
(1st Marquis of As-   Henriquez (Admiral).
torga). Ob. 1471.

Pedro Alvarez Osorio == Beatriz de Quiñones.
(2d Marquis of As-
torga). Ob. 1505.

Alvaro Perez Osorio == 1st. Isabel Sarmiento,
(3d Marquis of As-   Countess of Sta Marta.
torga). Ob. 1523.   2d. Mencia Osorio.

Pedro Alvarez Osorio == Maria Pimentel, d. of the
(4th Marquis of As-   Count of Benavente.
torga). Ob. 1560.

Alvaro Perez Osorio == Beatriz   Alonzo Perez Osorio   Pedro == Constanza
(5th Marquis of Astorga.)   de   (7th Marquis of Astorga).   Osorio   de Castro
Ob. 1567.   Toledo.   Ob. 1592.   Osorio.

Antonio Pedro Alvarez Osorio
(6th Marquis of Astorga).
Ob. 1589.

Pedro Alvarez Osorio == Blanca Manrique
(8th Marquis of Astorga).   y Aragon.
Ob. 1613.

Alvaro Perez Osorio   Constanza == Marquis of Keladar   ANA, *Countess of*
(9th Marquis of Astorga).   y San Roman.   *Chinchon.*

Leon—"a land of alpine passes, trout-streams, verdant meadows, and groves of chestnuts and walnuts"—to be married to Don Luis de Velasco, grandson of the first Marquis of Salinas, and the young couple went to live at Seville. This was in the year 1615.

Her husband's grandfather was a very great man indeed. He had been Viceroy of Mexico from 1589 to 1595, of Peru from 1595 to 1607, of Mexico a second time from 1607 to 1611, and was then President of the Council of the Indies at Seville. The old statesman died on September 7th, 1617, and the Lady Ana's husband succeeded him as second Marquis of Salinas. He was also Lord of Carrion, and a Knight of Santiago. The Lady Ana had children by her first husband. He died in the prime of life in 1619, and she lost her husband and her mother in the same year.

Thus, when little over twenty years old, still young and very beautiful, as her contemporaries tell us, the Lady Ana de Osorio became both a widow and an orphan. She was made a lady of the court to Margaret, the Queen of Felipe III., and removed from Seville to Madrid. Here she won the love of a nobleman of distinction, who possessed great estates in the neighbourhood—Don Luis Geronimo Fernandez de Cabrera y Bobadilla, fourth Count of Chinchon. His love was reciprocated, and the youthful widow was married a second time, at Madrid, on Sunday, August 11th, 1621.* The Lady Ana became Countess of Chinchon.

The Counts of Chinchon, whose first surname was Cabrera, were descended from a very ancient family of Catalonia,† whose history is given by Aragonese and Catalonian writers. Don Andres de Cabrera was Chamberlain to Enrique IV., and Alcaide of Segovia, the stronghold in which that king kept his treasure and jewels. Don Andres defended the Alcazar of Segovia against the rebels, and Enrique IV. granted him the estate of Moya as a reward in 1463. The town of Moya is a strong place on the confines of Castille and Aragon. Don Andres was also instrumental in effecting a reconciliation between Enrique and his sister Isabella, who met at a great banquet at Segovia in 1474. On the death of the King, Cabrera promptly delivered up the Alcazar, with all the arms and treasure, to Queen Isabella,

---

* *Blason España,* por Rivarola (1736), lib. iii. p. 302.

† *Estevan de Garibay, Compendio de España,* Pt. II. lib. xvii. cap. 2; *Pedro de Alcozer, Historia de Toledo,* cap. 115; *Geronimo de Zurita, Framentos manuscritos.*

in spite of the promises and bribes which were offered him by Alonzo of Portugal. His prompt loyalty was imitated by many nobles and prelates, and Fernando and Isabella were firmly seated on the throne. Don Andres Cabrera swore fealty on the day of Santa Lucia, and the grateful sovereigns decreed that on the anniversary of that day the golden cup out of which they and their successors drank should be sent as a present to Cabrera and his descendants for ever. Don Andres married the faithful attendant of Queen Isabella, Doña Beatriz Fernandez de Bobadilla, a lady of good family, whose ancestors were lords of the village of Boba-dilla, near Medina del Campo, in Castille; and her mistress granted the newly-married couple Chin-chon, Valdemoro, Casarubios, and seventeen other towns in the kingdom of Toledo, out of which the County was afterwards formed for their second son. Don Andres Cabrera was also created Marquis of Moya.

Doña Beatriz was a heroic champion and a most faithful friend to her royal mistress. When King Enrique was about to force his sister Isabella to marry Don Pedro Giron, the Master of Calatrava, Beatriz exclaimed, "God will not permit it, neither will I !"

D

then drawing forth a dagger from her bosom, she swore she would plunge it in his heart as soon as he appeared.* The Marquis and Marchioness of Moya accompanied their sovereigns in the campaign of Granada, and Queen Isabella recommended the companion of her youth to her successors when she died in 1504. The Marchioness, who was seldom separated from her royal mistress during life, had the melancholy satisfaction of closing her eyes in death. On the accession of Juana and Felipe, the Flemish favourites carried all before them, and the Moyas were forcibly expelled from Segovia; but, in 1506, the high-spirited Marchioness put herself at the head of a body of troops, and re-established herself in that strong fortress. She died soon afterwards, her husband, though much older, surviving her for a few years. They were both buried in the convent of the Order of Friars-Preachers at Carbonera, near Moya, which they themselves had founded.

Andres de Cabrera and Beatriz de Bobadilla were the illustrious progenitors of the Counts of Chinchon, who through them became hereditary Alcáides of Segovia.

---

* *Prescott's Ferdinand and Isabella,* vol. i. p. 138. The Master of Calntrava very opportunely died on the road.

The children of the first Marquis and Marchioness of Moya were as follows :—

1. Juan de Cabrera y Bobadilla, second Marquis of Moya. He married Ana de Mendoza, daughter of the first Duke of Infantado, by whom he had an only daughter, Luisa, Marchioness of Moya (ob. 1556). She married the Duke of Escalona, and had a daughter, Inez, married to the Count of Chinchon, and a son, Francisco Pacheco de Cabrera y Bobadilla, Duke of Escalona and Marquis of Moya. He married Juana de Toledo, daughter of the Count of Oropesa, and his second son, Francisco, became fifth Marquis of Moya. He married his cousin, Mencia, daughter of the third Count of Chinchon, A.D. 1615.

2. Hernando de Cabrera y Bobadilla, first Count of Chinchon, of whom presently.

3. Francisco de Cabrera y Bobadilla, Bishop of Salamanca.

4. Diego de Cabrera y Bobadilla, a Friar of the Order of Preachers. He had previously assisted his brother, the first Count of Chinchon, in defending Segovia against the *Comunidades* with great valour.

5. Pedro de Cabrera y Bobadilla, died off the

coast of Bretagne in 1521, when in command of the fleet of the Emperor Carlos V.

6. Maria, married to Don Pedro Manrique, Count of Osorno, but died childless.

7. Juana, also died childless.

8. Isabella, married to Don Diego Hurtado de Mendoza, Marquis of Cañete, and became mother of the Marquis who was Viceroy of Peru.

Arms of Cabrera y Bobadilla,

COUNTS OF CHINCHON.

Per pale : dexter, in chief, the royal lion and castle, in base on a field or a goat surrounded by a battlemented bordure sable for CABRERA : *sinister : quarterly, first and fourth a castle sable in flames on a field argent : second and third an eagle argent on a field gules, for* BOBADILLA : *the whole surrounded by an orle of royal lions and castles.*

III.

Counts of Chinchon.

ERNANDO DE CABRERA Y BOBA-DILLA, the second son of the first Marquis and Marchioness of Moya, was created Count of Chinchon by the King and Emperor Carlos I. and V. in the year 1517.* He was also Lord of the *sesmos* (districts) of Valdemoro, Casarubios, and eighteen other towns in the kingdom of Toledo, and was a Knight of the Order of Santiago.

The first Count of Chinchon distinguished himself in the revolt of the *Comunidades* in 1520. The original cause of the rebellion was, as is well known, that the Cortes assembled in Galicia voted Carlos I. a *free gift* on his accession, without obtaining the redress of a single grievance. The people of Toledo,

---

* *Berni, Titulos de Castilla* (Valencia, 1769), p. 205. Madoz says 1475, which is an error.

headed by their gallant young champion, Don Juan
de Padilla, seized the Alcazar, established a popular
form of government, and levied troops.   Segovia
followed the example of Toledo, as did Burgos,
Zamora, and other cities.   The people of Segovia,
reinforced and led by Padilla, repulsed the troops
sent against them by the Regent Adrian, and soon
afterwards the mad Queen Juana fell into the hands
of the rebels, and gave a colour of authority to their
proceedings.   Padilla was looked upon as the de-
liverer of the people.

During these troubles the Count of Chinchon successfully defended the strong *Alcazar* of Segovia, in
spite of the numerous assaults of the citizens.   After
the first outbreak, he left the fortress in charge of
his gallant brother, Diego de Cabrera, and set out
for his own estates near Madrid and Toledo, to col-
lect men and material.   He took all his artillery,
arms, and provisions from his Castle of Chinchon, and,
with a large body of servants and retainers, returned
to reinforce his brother.   Segovia was in the hands
of the rebels, and the *Alcazar* was closely besieged,
but the Count fought his way in, and brought
very timely succour.   Meanwhile, his own castle
at Chinchon was left without defence, and was

levelled to the ground by Padilla and the *Comuneros.**

As a reward for these ·services, the Counts of
Chinchon were made hereditary Alcaides of the
Alcazar of Segovia.

The first Count of Chinchon married Doña Teresa
de la Cueva, daughter of the second Duke of
Albuquerque, by whom he had two sons and a
daughter :—

1. Pedro Fernandez de Cabrera y Bobadilla,
second Count of Chinchon.

2. Andres de Cabrera, Bishop-elect of Carta-
gena.

3. Mariana, married to Don Luis de Leyva,
Prince of Asculi.

The first Count also had a natural son named
Pedro, who ' was a Franciscan Friar, and became
Provincial of the Order.

Don Pedro Fernandez de Cabrera y Bobadilla
succeeded his father as second Count of Chinchon.†
He served under Carlos I. in his wars, and
especially in the attack on Algiers; and he ac-

---

* *Cronica del Emperador Don Carlos*, lib. v. p. 132 ; *Nobiliario de
Haro*, Pt. I. lib. vii. cap. 3, p. 157.
† He was born at Chinchon (Madoz).

companied Felipe II. to England when he went to marry Queen Mary. In November 1554, when the Parliament of England petitioned for a reconciliation with Rome, Felipe sent the Count of Chinchon as his Ambassador from London, to announce the good news to Pope Paul IV. From this time the Count continued to be one of Felipe's most trusted ministers. He was a member of the Councils of State, of War, of Aragon, and of Italy, and Treasurer of the Crown of Aragon. ·

The second Count of Chinchon married Doña Mencia de la Cerda y Mendoza, daughter of Don Diego Hurtado de Mendoza, Count of Melito, by whom he had :—

1. Diego Fernandez de Cabrera y Bobadilla, third Count of Chinchon.

2. Andres de Cabrera, Bishop of Segovia, and afterwards Archbishop of Zaragoza.

3. Pedro de Cabrera, a distinguished soldier, who served in the expedition to succour Masalquivir in 1563, and was killed in action when La Goleta was lost.

4. Ana de Cabrera, died a Maid of Honour in the Palace.

5. Mencia de Cabrera, married Don Fernando

Cortes, Marquis of Valle, grandson of the Conqueror of Mexico, but died childless on July 1st, 1618.

6. Teresa de Cabrera y de la Cerda, married Don Pedro Fernandez de Castro, Count of Lemos. She was his second wife, and had two sons :—

1. Andres, whose only daughter, Francesca, eventually succeeded a cousin as eighth and last Countess of Chinchon. She married Don Enrique de Benavides, but had no children.

2. Rodrigo was in Peru with his cousin, the Viceroy, Count of Chinchon, as Governor of Chucuito. He afterwards entered holy orders, was a Canon of Toledo, and a Councillor of the Inquisition. (See page 37.)

Don Diego Fernandez de Cabrera y Bobadilla succeeded his father as third Count of Chinchon. He was at the battle of St Quentin, and in most of the other wars of the reign of Felipe II., and in 1593 he was employed, with Don Francisco de Mendoza, the Admiral of Aragon, in the expulsion of the Moriscos.* He was also a Knight of Santiago, a Councillor of State, and high in the confidence of Felipe II. The Castle of Chinchon had been de-

---

* *Nobiliario de Haro*, Pt. I. lib. v. cap. 5, p. 371.

F.

stroyed by the *Comuneros* in the time of his grand-father, and nothing remains of it but the splendid family chapel, now used as a parish church.   He, therefore, erected a new and very handsome castle, at great expense, on a hill to the south of the town of Chinchon, which I shall describe further on.   It now forms a very picturesque ruin.

The third Count of Chinchon married Doña Inez Pacheco, daughter of Don Diego Lopez Pacheco, Marquis of Villena and Duke of Escalona, by his wife Doña Luisa de Cabrera y Bobadilla, heiress of the Marquisate of Moya.   (See page 27.)   Their children were :—

1. Don Luis Geronimo Fernandez de Cabrera y Bobadilla, fourth Count of Chinchon.

2. Mencia de Cabrera, married her cousin, the Marquis of Moya.   (See page 27.)

3. Maria de Cabrera, married the fifth Marquis of Cañete.

4. Luisa de Cabrera, died childless.

IV.

€ije ffourtij €ount of €ijtncijon,

VICEROY OF PERU.

DON LUIS GERONIMO FERNANDEZ DE CABRERA Y BOBADILLA succeeded his father as fourth Count of Chinchon, Lord of Valdemoro and Casarubios, and hereditary Alcaide of Segovia. He was also a member of the Councils of Aragon and Italy, and Treasurer of the Crown of Aragon, and was about thirty years of age at the death of his father in 1619.

The fourth Count of Chinchon, as has already been mentioned, married the Lady Ana de Osorio, widow of the Marquis of Salinas, at Madrid, on Sunday (or, as some authorities say, Wednesday), the 11th of August 1621.

The Count and Countess resided, when not in attendance at Court, at Segovia or Chinchon. On Wednesday, September 13th, 1623, they entertained

Prince Charles (afterwards Charles I. of England) and the Duke of Buckingham at the Alcazar of Segovia, when, says the record, " they supped on certaine trouts of extraordinary greatnesse." [*]

In 1628 the Count of Chinchon was appointed Viceroy of Peru, the greatest and most important trust that could be conferred upon a subject, for in those days the Viceroyalty of Peru included the whole of South America, excepting Brazil. The Count and Countess went out by way of Panama, landed at Callao in December, and made their solemn entry into Lima on the 14th of January 1629, when the new Viceroy received the command from his predecessor, the Marquis of Guadalcazar. In the same year there was a terrible earthquake at Lima, which, though not to be compared in horror with the awful catastrophe of 1746, is said to have destroyed half the city.

The chief events of the Count of Chinchon's Viceroyalty were the rebellion in the Collao, the navigation of the Amazon, and the discovery of Peruvian bark.

On the western shores of the great lake of Titicaca

---

* Ford, vol. ii. p. 770.

there are thick beds of rushes, several leagues in
extent, in the midst of which there was an island,
inhabited by Ochozuma Indians, who made secret
lanes through the rushes, which they navigated in
their *balsas.* Secure in their lacustrine retreat, these
Indians committed many robberies on the highroad
from Chucuito to La Paz, until, in 1632, the Count
of Chinchon sent Don Rodrigo de Castro with a
small force to chastise them, and five of their chiefs
were taken prisoners, and hanged in the plaza of
Zepita. The head of one of them, named Juan
Pachacayo, was stuck on the bridge of the Desaguadero.

This only infuriated the Indians. They elected a
fierce and audacious man, named Pedro Laime, in
his place, who suddenly attacked the bridge of the
Desaguadero, burnt some houses, and carried off the
head of Pachacayo. The Spanish Corregidor or
Governor of Chucuito, the province on the western
shore of Lake Titicaca, was then Don Rodrigo de
Castro, a first cousin of the Viceroy, Count of Chinchon, being a son of his aunt, the Countess of Lemos.
(See page 33.) He collected some troops, and
marched along the shores of the lake, while the
rebels kept near him in their *balsas* in the rushes.

He addressed them, asking them to return to their allegiance, but was answered by jeers and shouts of defiance. He then advanced into the reedy swamp and opened fire upon them, occupying five islets amongst the rushes, near the mouth of the river Callacame. His soldiers burnt seventy huts, and carried off seven hundred head of cattle, but retired without discovering the concealed fastness of the Indians. The Count of Chinchon then gave orders that the Spaniards should embark on the lake, and on December 2d, 1632, the soldiers, forty in number, were put on board twenty *balsas.* On the 6th they came in sight of seventy *balsas,* under Pedro Laime, forming the hostile squadron. But the Indians went in and out amongst the rushes, by winding lanes of water only known to themselves, and baffled the efforts of the Spaniards to overtake them. They surprised one *balsa,* and killed the two soldiers in it, the others retreating. Next morning a party of cavalry followed some armed Indians into the swamp, and were suddenly surrounded. The Spaniards lost eleven men, and the Indians only three. The Ochozuma rebels then became bolder, and marched towards Zepita, which is the nearest town, but they were repulsed by Castro, who took seventeen prisoners, and sent them to the galleys at Callao. They, however, escaped on the road. Tranquillity was not completely restored until 1634; and the Viceroy acknowledged that the insurrection was caused by the injustice and tyranny of the Spaniards, who forced the Indians to work without pay, and seized on their goods.*

The memorable navigation of the river Amazon took place during the Viceroyalty of the Count of Chinchon. In 1637, two monks descended the rivers Napo and Amazon, and reached Pará. On their arrival, an expedition was sent up the river, commanded by Pedro de Texeira, which arrived at Quito in 1638. It was then proposed that Father Cristoval de Acuña, who was Rector of the College at Cuenca, should accompany Texeira on his return down the Amazon, and prepare a careful report of all that he might see. The matter was referred by the Judges of the Audiencia of Quito to the Count of Chinchon, who, after consulting the most eminent persons in Lima, sent orders to the President of Quito, in a letter dated November 1638, that Texeira, with all his people, should return to

---

* *Cronica Moralizada de la Provincia de Peru del Orden de San Agustin,* por el Padre Fray Antonio de la Calancha (Lima, 1653).

Pará. He likewise directed that two learned persons should accompany him, who might give an account of all that had been discovered, and that might be discovered on the return voyage. Two priests, named Cristoval de Acuña and Andres de Artieda, were selected; and a most valuable and useful book was the result of the Count of Chinchon's judicious order.*

But the most notable historical event in this Viceroy's time was the cure of his Countess, in the year 1638, of a tertian fever, by the use of Peruvian bark. The news of her illness at Lima reached Don Franciso Lopez de Cañizares, who was then Corregidor of Loxa, and who had become acquainted with the febrifuge virtues of the bark. I have convinced myself that the remedy was unknown to the Indians in the time of the Yncas. It is mentioned neither by the Ynca Garcilasso nor by Acosta, in their lists of Indian medicines, nor is it to be found in the wallets of itinerant native doctors, whose *materia medica* has been handed down from father to son for centuries. It appears, however, to have been known to the

---

* *El nuevo descubrimiento del gran rio de las Amazonas*, por el Padre Cristoval de Acuña (Madrid, 1641). Translated and edited, with notes, by Clements R. Markham (Hakluyt Society), 1859, p. 57.

Indians round Loxa, a town in the Andes, about 230 miles south of Quito. A Jesuit is said to have been cured of fever at Malacotas, near Loxa, by taking the bark given to him by the Indians, as long ago as 1600, and in about 1636 an Indian of Malacotas revealed the secret virtues of the *quiñquina* bark to the Corregidor Cañizares. In 1638, therefore, he sent a parcel of it to the Vice-Queen, and the new remedy, administered by her physician, Dr Don Juan de Vega, effected a rapid and complete cure. It is known by tradition amongst the bark collectors, that the particular species from which the bark was taken which cured the Countess of Chinchon, was that known to them as *Cascarilla* (bark) *de Chahuarguera.** These trees are a variety of the *C. officinalis* of Linnæus, hundreds of thousands of which are now growing in India, having been successfully introduced from the forests of Loxa. There are four alkaloids, with febrifuge virtues, in the Peruvian bark—quinine, quinidine, chinchonine, and chinchonidine. The *Cascarilla de Chahuarguera* abounds in chinchonidine, and Mr Howard has

---

* *Compendio Historico-medico-comercial de las Quinas,* por Don Hipolito Ruiz, MS. Quoted by Mr Howard in his *Nueva Quinologia de Pavon.*

F

pointed out* that this alkaloid probably contributed
to the cure of the Countess. It is now understood
that owing to its being at the same time as efficacious
as and much cheaper than quinine, the chinchonidine
will eventually be the chief agent by which health
and the cure of fevers will be diffused among the
vast native population of British India.

Madame de Genlis wrote a short novel, founded
on the cure of the Countess of Chinchon, which she
dedicated to the Comtesse de Choiseul. It is entitled "*Zuma,*" and though utterly wrong so far as
all the facts are concerned, and showing absolute
ignorance of Peru and even of Indian names, it yet
proves the deep and general interest which attaches
to the first introduction of *quina* bark into Europe
by the Vice-Queen.

The story, as told by Madame de Genlis, is briefly
as follows :—

"When the Count and Countess of Chinchon arrived in Peru, the
Indians felt an intense hatred for their Spanish oppressors. They
held a secret meeting on the hill where the *trees of health*, as they
called the *quina* trees, grew, and their leaders made them swear never
to divulge the secret of the healing virtue of the bark to the Spaniards ;
any one who did so was to be killed, with all his or her relations.
The Indian chiefs were named Azan, a fierce and cruel man ; Jimeo,

---

* Letter from Mr Howard to Mr Clements R. Markham, October
21st, 1873.

and his son Mirvan. The young chief Mirvan was married to a lovely girl named Zuma, and they had one child.

"When the Countess of Chinchon entered Lima, a band of girls with garlands of flowers, headed by Zuma, was forced to meet her. The Countess was so struck by Zuma's beauty, that she took her into the palace as an attendant. Four months afterwards the Countess was attacked by fever, and was on the point of death. Her Spanish maid, Beatriz, suspected Zuma of poisoning her, and set spies to watch her movements. Soon afterwards Zuma also fell ill of fever, and her husband got permission from the Indians to take her one dose of the *quina* bark every day. Zuma resolved to save the Countess and to die herself. Beatriz had told her suspicions to the Viceroy, and one night, while they were watching, they saw Zuma go stealthily into the Countess's room and put some powder into her medicine. The Viceroy rushed in, Zuma fainted, the bottle was broken, and she was sent to prison, accused of poisoning the Countess. Mirvan resolved to die with her, and gave himself up as an accomplice. They were tried and sentenced to be burnt alive, the Countess's physician deposing that her illness was mysterious, and that Zuma's powder was no doubt a deadly poison.

"The Countess was not told of Zuma's arrest until the morning appointed for the execution. She disbelieved her attendant's guilt. Dying as she was, she had herself carried to the place where the fire was lighted, ordered Mirvan and Zuma to be released, and brought them home with her. Soon afterwards the Viceroy, followed by the old chief, Jimeo, rushed into the Countess's room, and announced that the Indians had divulged the healing virtues of the *quina* bark, in order to save the lives of Zuma and her husband. The Countess was cured in eight days, Zuma was rewarded, and they all lived very happily ever afterwards." *

---

* Madame de Genlis's novel was translated into Spanish in 1827, and forms a little book entitled "*Zuma, ò el descubrimiento de la Quina, novelda Peruana.*"

At the end of his viceregal term, the Count of Chinchon was relieved by Don Pedro de Toledo y Leyva, Marquis of Mancera, who made his public entry into Lima on December 18th, 1639.

A very full account of the government of the Count of Chinchon was written by Dr Ocampo, the Archbishop of Lima, but it is still buried amongst the archiepiscopal archives. There is another relic of this Viceroy's administration in the shape of a *Sumario* or *précis*, written by Don José Caceres, the Secretary of his Government, on the case of a certain Don Manuel Criado de Castilla Ynca, a descendant of Manço Ynca, who so gallantly besieged the Spanish invaders in Cuzco; but this also is still in manuscript.*

The Countess of Chinchon returned to Spain in the spring of 1640, with her husband, and bringing with her a supply of that precious *quina* bark which had worked so wonderful a cure upon herself, and the healing virtues of which she intended to distribute amongst the sick on her lord's estates, and to make known generally in Europe. The bark

---

* *Gazofilacio Real Peruano*, por Don Gaspar de Escalona ; *Memorias de los Vireyes que han gobernado el Peru*, por M. A. Fuentes (Lima, 1859); p. xix.

powder was most appropriately called Countess's powder (*Pulvis Comitissæ*), and by this name it was long known to druggists and in commerce. Dr Don Juan de Vega, the learned physician * of the Countess of Chinchon, followed his patient to Spain, bringing with him a quantity of *quina* bark, which he sold at Seville at 100 reals the pound. The bark continued to have the same high value and the same reputation, until the trees became scarce, and the collectors began to adulterate it.

After their return from Peru, the Count and Countess of Chinchon usually resided at the Castle of Chinchon, which was built by the Count's father in about 1590. The Countess administered Peruvian bark to the sufferers from tertian agues on her lord's estates, in the fertile but unhealthy *vegas* of the Tagus, the Jarama, and the Tajuña. She thus spread blessings around her, and her good deeds are even now remembered by the people of Chinchon and Colmenar, in local traditions.†

* Dr Juan de Vega, while at Lima, published a grammar of the language of the Peruvian Indians, entitled "*Arte e Rudimentos de Gramatica Quichua.*" Impreso en Lima, 1636.

† Information from Don Hippolito Serrano, Regidor of Chinchon. When Carlos II. was given up in 1696, Mr Stanhope, the British Minister at Madrid, in a letter to Lord Lexington, said that " His

I have not been able to ascertain the dates on which the fourth Count of Chinchon and his Countess, the Lady Ana, died. I think that the Count died first; because I found a house in Chinchon with the arms of Osorio and Cabrera carved over the doorway, which may have been the dower-house of the widowed Countess.

They were succeeded by their son, the fifth Count, who was followed successively by two sons, the sixth and seventh Counts. Here the male line ended. The title was next inherited by their cousin, the Lady Francesca de Castro (see page 33), who became eighth Countess of Chinchon; but she died without issue, and the family came to an end. The Alcazar of Segovia, of which the Counts of Chinchon had long been hereditary Alcaides, was ceded to the Crown in the year 1764.

After the extinction of this grand old family, their title was dragged through the mud by the Bourbon kings. Carlos III. *sold* it to his brother, the Infante Felipe, Duke of Parma, and afterwards another of his brothers, the Infante Luis, bought the title of Count of Chinchon, with the estates attached

Catholic Majesty is now much better by taking the *quinquina.*"—*Lord Mahon's Spain under Charles II.*, p. 99.

to it. The illegitimate daughter of the Infante Luis was allowed to inherit this now degraded title, and she conveyed it to her husband, the notorious Manuel Godoy, Prince of Peace. Their daughter lived at Rome, and married the Duke of Alcudia, by whom she left a son, the present Count of Chinchon, and lord of the estates of Chinchon and Villaviciosa. He resides in Italy.

We find mention of Chinchon in history, during the War of the Succession. In the early part of 1706 Lord Peterborough had gained Valencia, Felipe V. had been repulsed before Barcelona and driven into France, and the incompetent Lord Galway, with the Portuguese General, Das Minas, had occupied Madrid. The allies seemed to be carrying all before them, but the fatal procrastination of the Archduke Charles and his Germans ruined these fair prospects. Lord Peterborough, the most brilliant statesman and soldier of his age, retired from Spain in disgust, Galway evacuated Madrid, and the allies, the English commanded by General Stanhope, took up their quarters in the town of Chinchon, in August. Meanwhile, the Duke of Berwick had assumed the command of Felipe's troops, armed bodies of peasants from La Mancha lined the south banks of the Tagus,

cutting off the retreat of the allies to Portugal, and
the allied Generals remained at Chinchon, wavering
and procrastinating. In a letter dated from Chinchon on August 22d, General Stanhope says that he
cannot venture to attempt the passage of the Jarama
before such an enemy as Berwick; that the country
of Castille is daily falling from the allies, and that
they can only reckon themselves masters of the
ground they encamp on. General Stanhope wrote
another letter from Chinchon to the Lord Treasurer,
dated August 25th, complaining of the undisciplined
and penniless condition of the Portuguese contin-
gent. During their stay at Chinchon they were often
pinched for want of provisions, owing to the unfriend-
liness of the country, and hardly a straggler could
leave the town without being seized or murdered. At
length, in September, the allies began their march from
Chinchon, and crossed the Tagus at Fuentidueña,
followed by Berwick, retreating hastily into Valencia,
where they took up their winter quarters.*

Afterwards Felipe V. passed a night at Chinchon,
and the house in which he slept is still shown.

During the Peninsular War, Chinchon suffered

---

* *Lord Mahon's War of the Succession in Spain*, chap. v. p. 216;
Letters from General Stanhope, p. xxxi.

cruelly from the depredations of the French. The old castle was dismantled and ruined, the church, excepting the tower, was levelled with the ground,* and the townspeople were ruthlessly massacred for having shown some slight intention of resisting a French advanced guard.

---

* Set on fire, by order of Marshal Victor, on Dec. 27th, 1810 (Madoz). It had been endowed by the Count of Chinchon in 1589; rebuilt, 1819–28.

CABRERA Y BOBADILLA,

Marquises of Moya and Counts of Chinchon.

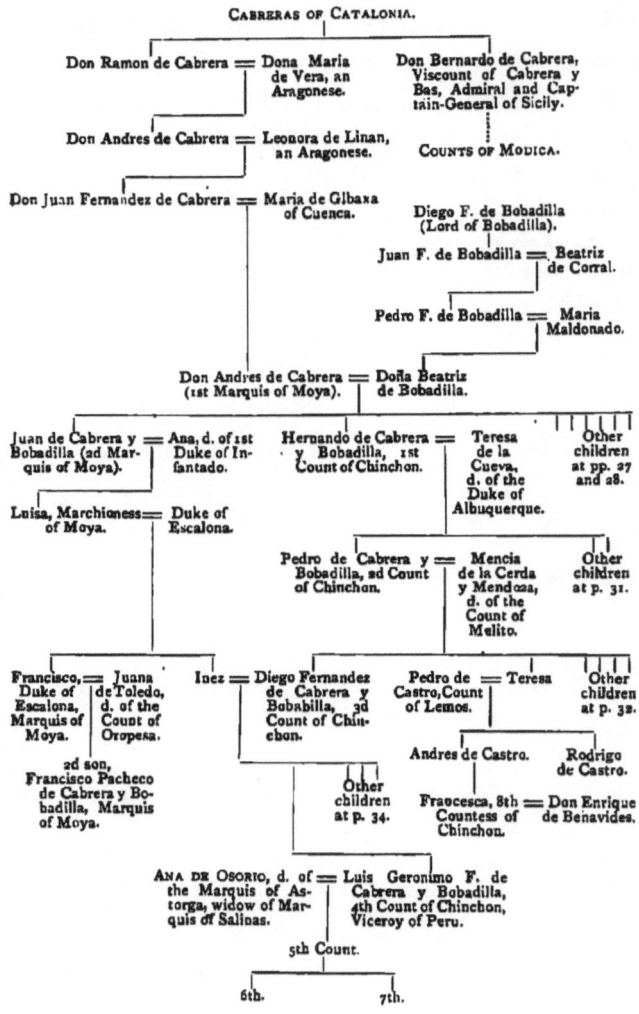

CABRERAS OF CATALONIA.

Don Ramon de Cabrera == Dona Maria de Vera, an Aragonese.

Don Bernardo de Cabrera, Viscount of Cabrera y Bas, Admiral and Captain-General of Sicily.

Don Andres de Cabrera == Leonora de Linan, an Aragonese.

COUNTS OF MODICA.

Don Juan Fernandez de Cabrera == Maria de Gibaxa of Cuenca.

Diego F. de Bobadilla (Lord of Bobadilla).

Juan F. de Bobadilla == Beatriz de Corral.

Pedro F. de Bobadilla == Maria Maldonado.

Don Andres de Cabrera == Doña Beatriz de Bobadilla.
(1st Marquis of Moya).

Juan de Cabrera y Bobadilla (2d Marquis of Moya). == Ana, d. of 1st Duke of Infantado.

Hernando de Cabrera y Bobadilla, 1st Count of Chinchon. == Teresa de la Cueva, d. of the Duke of Albuquerque.

Other children at pp. 27 and 28.

Luisa, Marchioness of Moya. == Duke of Escalona.

Pedro de Cabrera y Bobadilla, 2d Count of Chinchon. == Mencia de la Cerda y Mendoza, d. of the Count of Melito.

Other children at p. 31.

Francisco, Duke of Escalona, Marquis of Moya. == Juana de Toledo, d. of the Count of Oropesa.

2d son, Francisco Pacheco de Cabrera y Bobadilla, Marquis of Moya.

Inez == Diego Fernandez de Cabrera y Bobabilla, 3d Count of Chinchon.

Pedro de Castro, Count of Lemos. == Teresa.

Other children at p. 32.

Andres de Castro.

Rodrigo de Castro.

Other children at p. 34.

Francesca, 8th Countess of Chinchon. == Don Enrique de Benavides.

ANA DE OSORIO, d. of the Marquis of Astorga, widow of Marquis of Salinas. == Luis Geronimo F. de Cabrera y Bobadilla, 4th Count of Chinchon, Viceroy of Peru.

5th Count.

6th.   7th.

SEIZE QUARTIERS OF ANA DE OSORIO,

COUNTESS OF CHINCHON, VICE-QUEEN OF PERU.

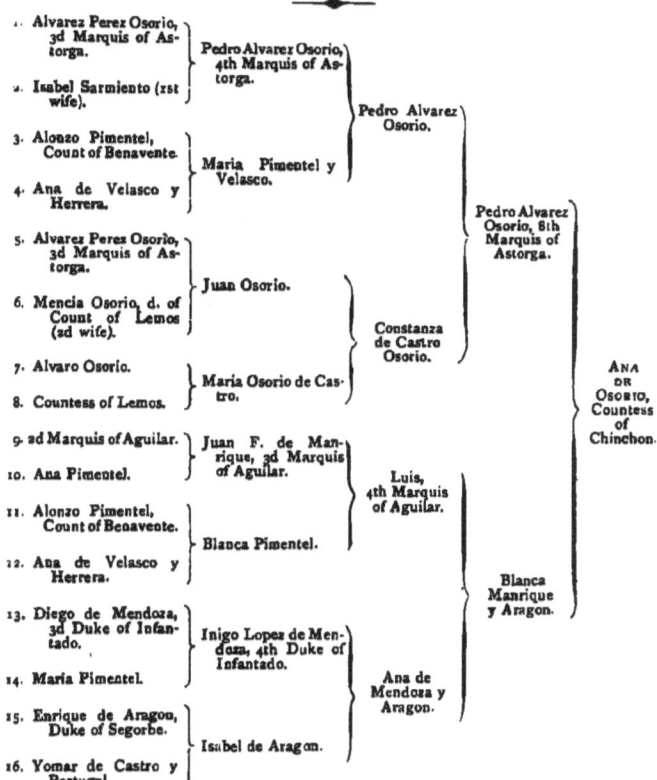

1. Alvarez Perez Osorio, 3d Marquis of Astorga.

2. Isabel Sarmiento (1st wife).

— Pedro Alvarez Osorio, 4th Marquis of Astorga.

3. Alonzo Pimentel, Count of Benavente.

4. Ana de Velasco y Herrera.

— Maria Pimentel y Velasco.

— Pedro Alvarez Osorio.

5. Alvarez Perez Osorio, 3d Marquis of Astorga.

6. Mencia Osorio, d. of Count of Lemos (2d wife).

— Juan Osorio.

7. Alvaro Osorio.

8. Countess of Lemos.

— Maria Osorio de Castro.

— Constanza de Castro Osorio.

— Pedro Alvarez Osorio, 8th Marquis of Astorga.

9. 2d Marquis of Aguilar.

10. Ana Pimentel.

— Juan F. de Manrique, 3d Marquis of Aguilar.

11. Alonzo Pimentel, Count of Benavente.

12. Ana de Velasco y Herrera.

— Blanca Pimentel.

— Luis, 4th Marquis of Aguilar.

13. Diego de Mendoza, 3d Duke of Infantado.

14. Maria Pimentel.

— Inigo Lopez de Mendoza, 4th Duke of Infantado.

15. Enrique de Aragon, Duke of Segorbe.

16. Yomar de Castro y Portugal.

— Isabel de Aragon.

— Ana de Mendoza y Aragon.

— Blanca Manrique y Aragon.

— ANA DE OSORIO, Countess of Chinchon.

CHINCHON. (*From the Castle Hill.*)

V.

Chinchon.

THE province of Madrid, in New Castille, is in the very centre of Spain, and the pillar marking the actual centre may be seen from the hills above Chinchon. Modern tourists tell us little that is new, still less that is correct. Those who go to Spain generally announce, in a sprightly off-hand way, that Madrid is surrounded by an arid desert. This is not the truth, nor anything at all near it.

The province of Madrid is situated between 39°

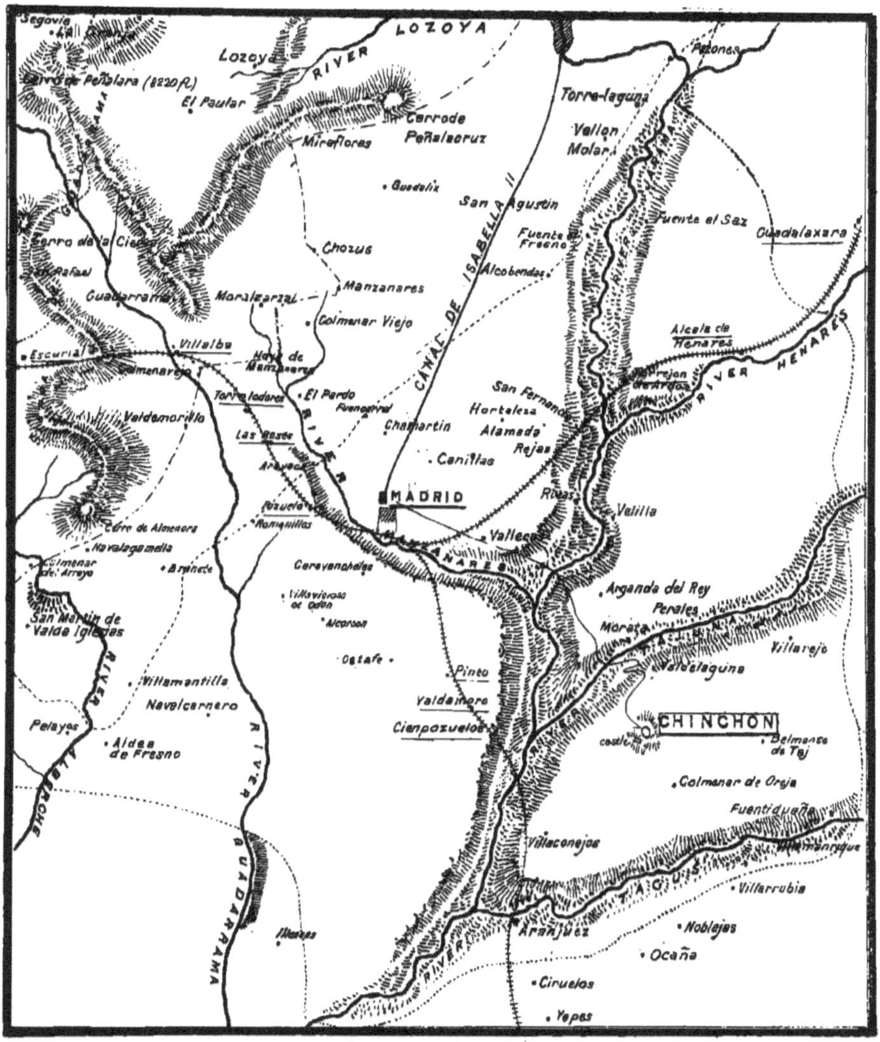

THE PROVINCE OF MADRID

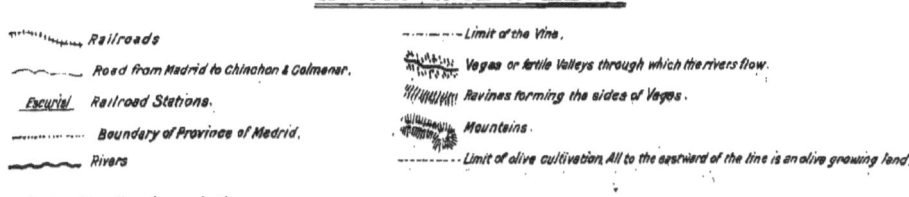

Railroads

Road from Madrid to Chinchon & Colmenar.

Escurial Railroad Stations.

Boundary of Province of Madrid.

Rivers

Scale 10 miles to an inch

Limit of the Vine.

Vegas or fertile Valleys through which the rivers flow.

Ravines forming the sides of Vegas.

Mountains.

Limit of olive cultivation. All to the eastward of the line is an olive growing land.

53′ and 41° 7′ N. lat., and consists of a tableland intersected by deep valleys. It covers an area of about 250 square leagues. The elevation above the sea varies from 1500 in the valleys to 8500 feet on the summits of the Guadarrama peaks. This range of mountains extends along the northern and western sides of the province, and though no part of it rises above the line of perpetual snow, the snow lies in some sheltered corners until July, and falls again early in October. The lower slopes of the Guadarramas are clothed with oaks, above which various species of conifers extend as high as to 6500 feet above the sea, with yews and junipers. The *Pinus sylvestris* (Scotch Pine) is a fine tree, with spreading branches drooping to the ground, which clothes the sides of the Peñalara peak, overhanging the summer palace of La Granja. *Pinus pinea* (Stone Pine) is a beautiful tree, which forms the groves of San Martin de Valdeiglesias ; and the *Pinus pinaster* (Cluster Pine) is also common in the Guadarramas. These mountains are formed of white granite ; the rest of the province, with the exception of small Cretacean and Silurian patches in the north, being of Tertiary formation.

The rivers of the province are the Alberche and Guadarrama, flowing from the mountains direct to the Tagus; the Manzanares and Lozoya also flowing from the Guadarramas and falling into the Jarama; and the Jarama, Henares, and Tajuña coming from the eastward, uniting with each other, and falling into the Tagus (which river forms the southern boundary of the province) near Aranjuez.

Eastward of the Guadarrama mountains, the province of Madrid consists of a rolling tableland covered with corn, olives, and vines, but generally treeless, and towards its eastern frontier some wild barren mountains rise up along the Guadalaxara frontier. The tableland is, however, intersected by deep valleys, through which the rivers flow, of great fertility, well wooded, and generally bounded by hills with scarped precipitous sides. Here the vineyards are intermixed with luxuriant fruit and vegetable gardens, while in some places there is a fine growth of trees. The well-grown timber and shady groves of San Fernando, San Martin de Valdeiglesias, and Aranjuez are the pride of the Madrileños, and especially the magnificent elms, brought from England by Felipe II., and planted at Aranjuez, are celebrated not only by Spaniards, but by our countryman, John Evelyn.[*]

---

[*] *Sylva*, Book I. chap. 7.

The chief products of the province, given in the order of their yield, are barley, wheat, wine, oats, olive oil, pulses, potatoes, hemp, flax, besides fruits and garden vegetables.*

The province is divided into eight *Cercados*, or *Partidos Judiciales*, for purposes of judicial and civil administration :—

1. Chinchon.
2. Getafe.
3. Navalcamero.
4. Madrid.
5. Alcala.
6. San Martin de Valdeiglesias.
7. Torrelaguna.
8. Colmenar Viejo.

The town of Chinchon is in the south-east corner of the province, on very high ground, with hills covered with wheat-fields, olives, and vineyards, sloping off on one side to the *vega* of the Tagus, and on the other to that of the Tajuña.

---

* According to Don Vicente Cutanda, the province of Madrid possesses a flora (exclusive of cryptogamia) consisting of 101 families, 609 genera, and 1867 species, and participating both in a Subalpine and a Mediterranean character.

Among ferns the *Gramitis Ceterach, Polypodium vulgare, Aspidium Felix mas, Asplenium trichomanes, Ruta-muraria, Septentrionale, Adiantum nigrum, Scolopendrium officinale, Pteris Aquilina* and *crispa, Adiantum Capillus Veneris,* and *Odorum,* are found in the Guadarramas (*Flora Compendiada de Madrid,* 1861).

An omnibus leaves the Calle de Alcala in Madrid, for Chinchon and Colmenar de Oreja, at eight o'clock every morning; and on that of the 21st of October 1866, I took my place in it, with two agreeable and communicative companions, one a stout, elderly renter of vineyards and dealer in brandy, who had been in London during the Exhibition of 1862, the other a young man in charge of the Chinchon prison, with a gun across his knees, and much talk touching the potting of doves and sparrows.

The distance from Madrid to Chinchon is twenty-four miles. The road leads down the Prado, and past the famous chapel of Atocha, and then becomes execrable for two or three miles, after which it is excellent for the rest of the distance. Crossing the Saragossa railroad, it passes through the large village of Vallecas, and descends into the *vega* of the Jarama, where the tableland ends abruptly in scarped and rugged cliffs, and where the rich fertility of the valley offers a strong contrast to the treeless expanse of corn-field and vineyard on the high ground. Crossing the river by a long bridge, the road leaves the valley by a steep ascent, passes over another stretch of tableland, and again descends into the larger and equally fertile *vega* of the Tajuña, at a point where the village of Morata is in sight, a mile or two up the river. These *vegas* are formed of a rich alluvial soil, and yield delicious melons, and indeed every kind of fruit and vegetable, but they are unhealthy—the haunts of ague and intermittent fever.

There are no country-houses, no detached cottages on this road. All the inhabitants live in the towns or large villages. This immemorial usage dates of course from the time when New Castille was the debatable ground between the Moors and Christians, and is now a necessity to the people, because all the habits and customs of their daily lives depend upon it. The unhealthiness of the *vegas*, in which much of the field-work lies, may also be one reason that the labourers all live in villages on the higher ground. So at early dawn the Castillian peasants, in their velveteen tufted bonnets, may be seen issuing from the towns, mounted on mules, with the day's provisions in their *alforjas*, and their simple ploughs and other implements drawn along behind. With a strict code of morals, such as it is, proud but courteous in his bearing, not wanting in intelligence, and exacting that respect from others which he justly

H

feels for himself, the Castillian peasant is far
superior to the agricultural labourer in England,
or indeed in any other part of Europe.   The
estates are large, and generally belong to some
grandee or rich proprietor, and the cultivators
rent their own land, nominally as tenants at will,
but really handing it down from father to son,
for generations.

There is a long suspension bridge over the

THE CASTLE OF CHINCHON.
(*South side.*)

formidable river Tajuña, and the road then leaves
the *vega*, ascends the hills by two zigzags, and
leads across another tableland to Chinchon.   The
ruined castle and large church are visible miles
away, on the tableland between the *vegas* of
Tajuña and Jarama.   The town lies in a slight

hollow, with the castle to the south, and the church, overhanging the houses, on the northern hill.

The ruins of the old Castle of Chinchon stand on a breezy hill, with the little town nestling at its feet on one side, and a wide view across the

ARMS OF THE COUNTS OF CHINCHON.
(Carved in stone over the drawbridge of the castle.)

vega of Tajuña on the other, ending in the distant peaks of the Guadarrama range. The soft velvety turf round the ruins is bordered by wheat-fields, which are succeeded, lower down the hillside, by vineyards and olive-trees.

The castle had once been a place of considerable strength, and also a very noble residence. The interior consists of a quadrangle with ramparts on three sides, underneath which are vaulted casemates suitable for storerooms, cellars, or barracks, and the castle itself forms the western side. It is now a complete ruin ; but the lofty windows, wide portals, and spacious well-proportioned rooms attest .its former magnificence. At each angle of the building there is a circular · tower, and three windows for each of the two stories are pierced in the intervening walls. The lower story, though appearing at a considerable height from the outside, is in reality on a level with the quadrangle.

The entrance into the castle is by a causeway over a wide arch spanning the ditch, at the end of which there was a drawbridge leading to the grand portal in the centre of the southern wall. Over the entrance a masonry wall was built for the chains of the drawbridge, and on its face the arms of Cabrera y Bobadilla are carved in bold relief, with a cross fleury behind them, and surmounted by a count's coronet and an eagle displayed, as a crest. This coat of arms proves the date at which the castle was built, for it has an escutcheon of pretence in the centre, bearing two caldrons.* Now these are the arms of the Duke of Escalona,† whose daughter Inez married the third Count of Chinchon.‡ He,

ENTRANCE TO THE CASTLE OF CHINCHON.
(*East side.*)

therefore, must have been the builder of the castle, towards the end of the reign of Felipe II; the more ancient castle on the other side of the town having been destroyed by the *Comuneros* in the time of his grandfather.§

---

* See page 3 and note.
† *Nobiliario de Haro*, II. lib ix. cap. 26.
‡ See page 34.
§ See pages 30 and 33.

The castle is built of Tertiary limestone, brought from the adjacent quarries of Colmenar Oreja;* and as no mosses or lichens form on the walls in this dry and bright climate, they look as new and fresh as when they were first built. This effect rather increases the idea of melancholy desolation, for it makes the ruins appear as if they had been bombarded and gutted but yester-day.

In this old castle the good Countess Ana lived, after her return from Peru; and from here she diffused blessings in every direction; not only administering her bark powders to the sick peasants in the adjacent *vegas,* and to the students at the University of Alcala; but communicating a knowledge of their virtues to the rest of the world, so that they were known throughout Chris-tendom as *Pulvera Comitissæ.*

On the hill which rises up in front of the castle, and quite overhanging the town, is the tower of the old parish church, every other part of which was destroyed by the French. An open space, with a parapet wall, overlooking the town, and a row of trees, intervenes between this tower and the old

* Ford, ii. p. 657.

family chapel of the counts, now used as the parish church. Here, on this pleasant eminence, all the people congregate on Sundays and *fiestas*, the old men sitting on the benches and smoking cigaritas, boys playing at skittles, and girls at hide-and-seek amongst the buttresses of the old chapel. Nearly

CHINCHON AND THE CASTLE.
(*From the hill on which the church stands.*)

all looked fresh and healthy, and an astonishing proportion have fair or red hair.*

The chapel is a very spacious and lofty building, but with no architectural pretension of any kind. It is dedicated to our Lady of the Assumption;

---

* The school was founded by Dr Antonio Alvarez Gato, in 1729.

and there is a tolerable picture of the Assumption over the high altar, said to be by Goya.* The three other pictures are of no merit—a *Santa Lucia,* a *San Augustin,* and a *Divina Pastora.* The family vault of the Counts of Chinchon is under the high altar, and there were formerly ten marble statues of Counts and Countesses of Chinchon in the church, but they were smashed into small pieces by the French soldiers. For many years the pieces were piled together, so as to form seats, in the court of a house a little higher up the hill, on the site of the old castle destroyed by the *Comuneros.* (See page 30.) Here the women and old people looked on, while the young men played matches at fives (*Juego de pelota*) ; for this place was long the fives-court of the townspeople. A few years ago the house changed hands, and the fives-court was abolished. The pieces of the statues were then carted away by the major-domo of the present Count, and stowed in one of the large chambers in the ditch of the castle. I

* Goya was a Spanish painter who flourished 1746–1828. Two of his pictures, *Queen Maria Luisa,* and a *Bull-fighter,* are in the Madrid gallery. Also *Stas. Justa* and *Rufina* in Seville Cathedral. He was also an etcher, and published some spirited caricatures.

rummaged amongst them, and found arms, hands, bits of drapery, coats of arms, mouldings, all of white marble, but not a single complete head or face.

The town of Chinchon lies in the hollow, and up the sides of the hills, on the crest of one of

POSADA DE LA ESQUINA.
(*In the Plaza. Chinchon.*)

which stands the old ruined castle, and on that of the other the tower and the church. The *plaza* is in the hollow, and its four sides are formed of two-storied houses, with balconies along both stories, as is essential in a country where every

I

village *plaza* is periodically converted into a bull-
ring.   On such occasions barriers are placed across
the streets at the corners, the whole population,
in gala attire, assembles in the balconies of the
plaza, and the young men exhibit their prowess
before their relations and townsmen, and above
all before those in whose eyes they desire to
stand well.   The bulls are not usually killed,
and there are none of the barbarous scenes which
are so common in the bull-rings of Madrid and
the   provincial   capitals.   The   village   youths
generally confine themselves to the work of the
picadores, but this involves no small amount of
pluck and agility, and is some sort of substitute
(a bad one, but better than none at all) for cricket
and football.

In one corner of the *plaza* is the inn, the "*Fonda
de la esquina*," as it is called, where the muleteers
put up.   But there are also two clean rooms for
visitors, and the landlady, a civil talkative old
housekeeper from Madrid, supplies a clean table-
cloth, fowls and eggs, white delicious bread,
excellent ham, Chinchon wine, and clean beds.
Would that all Spanish inns were like the humble.
little *fonda* at Chinchon!

HOUSE AT THE CORNER OF THE PLAZA.
(*Chinchon.*)

Shield of arms carved on a house in *Chinchon.*

Many of the houses in the streets of Chinchon have shields of arms carved in stone over the great doorways leading into the inner courts, or higher up between the windows. In these houses dwelt, in former days, the hidalgos or smaller gentry, who were, in some measure, the retainers of the great counts, who attended them at

Court and followed them in battle. Don Quijote himself was such an one ; living in a street in a village of

La Mancha, the name of which
Cervantes does not care to re-
member, but which others be-
lieve to have been Argamasilla
de Alba. If we may judge
from the number of shields
carved on the walls of houses,
the good town of Chinchon
was once well supplied with
those gentlemen of coat
armour, of whom the gallant
old knight of La Mancha is

Shield of arms carved on a house in
Chinchon.

the representative. But they have now passed away;
their descendants are probably loafing at Madrid,
and idling away their time in the Puerto del
Sol, while their houses are occupied by ordi-
nary *paisanos*. In the olden time, however, such
a place as Chinchon must have been gay and
bustling enough; with the miniature court of
its proud and wealthy Count at the castle on the
hill, houses of resident gentry in every street, a
vast monastery of Franciscans,* and a nunnery of

---

* Founded by the Count and Countess of Chinchon in 1606 ; and
completed by their grandson, who was buried there. (*Madoz.*)

the same order.   The castle is now a ruin, the
hidalgos are gone, the monastery has been converted into a prison, and the
nuns are reduced to five poor
creatures of a certain age, im-
mured in an enormous building,
and living exclusively on charity.

In the inner court of one
of the houses I found a slab of
white limestone, with an in-
scription.   I cannot make anything out of it, but I have
copied it because it bears a
date which is the year after
the Countess Ana returned from Peru to Chin-

JUAN   CARRASCO
Shield of arms carved on a house in
Chinchon.

chon, and records the memory of some one in
the town who was no doubt personally known to her.   The shield,
here sketched, is carved low down
on the wall in the same court.   It
indicates, I apprehend, that the house
was once the residence of a knight of
Calatrava.   A girl sat by a well in

TEJEDA
Shield of arms carved on
a house in *Chinchon.*

the court, under the shade of two fig-trees, singing
and broidering.   There is one other house deserving

of notice, at the corner of the street leading up
to the castle; for tradition relates that Felipe V.
passed a night in it, after the allies evacuated
Chinchon, during the War of Succession.

MARQUES DEL C....
Shield of arms carved on a house in
Chinchon.

Don Pedro Diaz, the ad-
ministrador or agent of the
Count's estates, and Don
Hippolito Serrano, one of
the Regidores of the Judge's
Court, were my principal in-
formants.   They estimated
the population of Chinchon
at 6000 souls,* in 1300
families. † Most of these
families are engaged in making wine and brandy.
The Chinchon wine is the same as Arganda, both
being a superior sort of Valdepeñas.   There is no large
manufactory, but each family makes its own wine, for
sale and home consumption, from its own vineyards.
The presses are in the inner courts of the houses,
and all the processes of wine-making are conducted
on the premises.   I was informed that 130,000 *arrobas*
of wine were made every year.   The brandy of

---

* Madoz says 5288, in 1850.   † Madoz says there are 984 houses.

Chinchon, made from the juice and not from the skin of the grapes, is renowned as the best in the Castilles. There are subterranean caves for storing the wine.

The cultivated fields and gardens, and many of the vineyards of the people of Chinchon are in the *vega* of the Tajuña, and the labourers have a long ride to their work, in a situation which exposes them to attacks of fever and ague. Hence the necessity for supplies of *quina* bark is as great now as it was in the days of the good Countess, though they are not now so plentifully or bountifully furnished. But the memory of the acts of the Countess Ana, of how she administered the fever-dispelling powders to the vassals of her husband, and spread the knowledge of them far and wide, is still cherished in Chinchon. The tradition was mentioned to me spontaneously, both by Serrano and Diaz.

And well has the fair Ana de Osorio merited these grateful memories. This distinguished lady was one of the most noble benefactors of the human race; and while she is remembered with blessings by the peasants of Castille, her name is most appropriately immortalised in the genus of inestimable plants, whose virtues she first made known.　Yet that honoured name is, through a misapprehension originated by Linnæus, frequently misspelt by modern writers.　It will be the object of the rest of this Memoir to show that the correct spelling ought to be adhered to.

VI.

𝔗𝔥𝔢 𝔠𝔥𝔦𝔫𝔠𝔥𝔬𝔫𝔞 𝔊𝔢𝔫𝔲𝔰.

𝕿HE Countess of Chinchon's powders continued to be imported into Europe for a century, and the beautiful trees whence the bark was taken were known as *quina* or *quinquina* trees. It was not until the French expedition of Condamine and Jussieu went to America in 1735, that the forests of Loxa were visited by scientific men, and a few years afterwards Condamine sent specimens of the *quinquina* plant to the great Swedish botanist Linnæus, who was the first to describe it. The name of a new and most important genus was then to be given by Linnæus, and he chose for it the most appropriate that could possibly have been selected, namely, that of the noble lady who had first made its healing virtues known. In 1742, Linnæus

K

gave the name of *Chinchona* to the genus,* with the intention of thus immortalising the great and beneficent acts of the *Countess of Chinchon.* Of course that intention is frustrated by spelling the name wrong.

But most unfortunately Linnæus was misinformed as to the name of her whom he desired to honour. This is to be accounted for by his having received his knowledge of the Countess of Chinchon through a French source, and French writers frequently alter the spelling of names that are not French.† Thus misled, Linnæus spelt the word *Cinchona* (*Gen. Pl.* 1742), and *Cinhona* (*Gen. Pl.* ed. 1767), omitting one or two letters; but the fact that he altered the spelling in his different editions, proves beyond any doubt that he desired to spell the word correctly.

It was still more unfortunate that Linnæus died before the error was pointed out and

---

* In the 2d ed. of his *Genera Plantarum,* from the figure and description by La Condamine in the *Mémoires de l'Académie de Paris,* 1738, p. 226.

† See *Mémoires de l'Académie* 1738, p. 226. See also the *Vie de la Fontaine* by Walckenaër, where the names are ruthlessly mutilated. We have *le Comte de Cinchon* and *la Comtesse de Cinchon!*

corrected. This was done by the Spanish botanists Ruiz and Pavon, who landed in Perú in 1778, the very year of Linnæus's death. They explored the forests of Huanuco and Loxa, discovered many new species of *Chinchonæ*, and are among the highest authorities on the subject. They strongly advocated the correct spelling of that genus to the study of which they had devoted so much time, and exposed themselves to so many hardships and dangers.

The botanist Mutis, with his disciples Zea and Caldas, were engaged in the study of the *Chinchonæ* of New Granada, the former residing in South America, chiefly at Bogota, from 1783, until his death in 1808. They also spelt the word correctly, as may be seen by their numerous reports and pamphlets on the subject.* They were followed by Cavanilles, Lagasca, Rodriguez, and other Spanish botanists, and the oversight of Linnæus was thus corrected.

---

* See the *Informe que dió el Dr Don Josef C. Mutis con motivo del descubrimiento de la quina de Santa Fé, hecho* por *Don Sebastian Josef Lopez Ruiz*, where the word is spelt correctly *Chinchona*. See also the *Memoria* by Don Francisco Antonio Zea. (Madrid, 1802.)

One would have supposed, when the original error had been corrected by all the great authorities who wrote upon the subject, immediately after the death of Linnæus, that the honoured name of the Countess Ana would have been safe from future mutilation, and that the correct spelling of the *Chinchona* genus would have been fully established. Yet this has not been the case. Humboldt and Bonpland, as well as Weddell and Karsten, have copied the unintentional error of Linnæus, instead of following the higher authority,\ on this particular point, of the great Spanish botanists who explored the Chinchona forests. A host of other writers have perpetuated the ill-omened mutilation of the Countess's name, calling the genus *Cinchona*, from *cinchon*, a policeman's belt, instead of *Chinchona*, from the *Countess of Chinchon.* It is now proposed to discontinue this omission of an important letter in the name.

When Mr Howard published his magnificent edition of the *Nueva Quinologia* of Pavon, he very properly retained the correct spelling of the word in the headings, and in the Latin descriptions of his author. In a note he says that

Pavon strongly pleads for the correct spelling, and adds that in his (Mr Howard's) opinion, he does so with justice.*

Dr Berthold Seemann, a German botanist who has himself visited the *Chinchona* forests of Loxa, also strongly advocates the correct spelling. He says in his *Journal of Botany* (i. p. 37, note), " Dr Hooker has drawn attention to the fact that Linnæus spelt this word not only *Cinchona*, but in the edition of 1767, *Cinhona*. Those who have hitherto objected to the correct spelling (*Chinchona*, because the genus was named after the *Countess of Chinchon*), on the plea that Linnæus wrote *Cinchona*, will see the impropriety of adhering any longer to that orthography."

Mr Spruce, the eminent botanist, whose name is connected with one of the most valuable of the *Chinchona* species, has also adopted the correct spelling.

As regards this question, the botanical authorities .

---

* *Nueva Quinologia, ó sea una Monografia de 41 especies de Quinas ó Cascarillas, cuyo genero en Botanica Chinchon.* Mr Howard says, " I have not found it possible to adhere strictly to the orthography of the word *Chinchona*, for which Pavon strongly, and *I think, with justice*, pleads, as being derived from the family name of *Chinchon*." Intr. p. ii. (note.)

who have visited the *Chinchona* forests, and have written on the genus, stand as follows :—

BOTANICAL AUTHORITIES WHO SPELL THE WORD CORRECTLY. (*Chinchona.*)	AUTHORITIES WHO SPELL THE WORD INCORRECTLY. (*Cinchona.*)
1. Pavon.	1. Humboldt and Bonpland.
2. Ruiz.	2. Bergen.
3. Tafalla.	3. Poeppig.
4. Mutis.	4. Weddell.
5. Zea.	5. Triana.
6. Caldas.	6. Karsten.
7. Seemann.	7. Delondre.
8. Spruce.	

Thus the spelling *Chinchona* is, beyond any doubt, correct, all other forms being wrong; it is adopted by the majority of authorities who have studied the genus in its native habitat, and it is now the form in common use where the plant is cultivated, and in official correspondence ; and is consequently the most convenient form.   Under these circumstances the burden of proof is clearly with those who advocate the spelling of the word incorrectly.

It is urged, on very high authority, as follows :—

" The expediency of changing the generic name from *Cinchona* to *Chinchona* is not so clear.   I really do not like to speak dogmatically, or think positively on it, for, like all other questions of spelling in nomenclature, it is not to be settled by *authority* nor by *right.*   I once was myself a purist, and insisted on the adoption

of the true spelling in similar cases, and found that I was not
followed, however right. Names are *means* not *ends*, and their
uses as means once established, it is all but impossible to alter
them. I speak from a very extended experience and much obser-
vation, without prejudice and with no predilection for *Cinchona*,
but quite the contrary. You are absolutely right in the abstract,
but *right* never ruled such cases, when once the wrong was
established. In nine cases out of ten it is kicking against the
pricks, and there are scores of similar cases in botany that
are spasmodically kicked against by great and good authorities,
and all to no purpose. Therefore the question turns wholly on
the two considerations—1st, which spelling will be followed in
future; 2d, if I adopt *Chinchona*, I must also alter a lot of other
names on the same ground, some of which have never yet been
altered and others have been altered repeatedly, to no purpose,
as far as getting the right spelling adopted. Then too there is
a serious practical consideration. An uninstructed man looks
for *Chinchona* in the Index under *Ci* not *Ch*, and not finding it,
he is thrown out. After all, the fact is that the world has accepted
Cinchona as the botanical equivalent of *Chinchona*, and that being
accepted, it is as well understood as *Vienna* for *Wien*, or *Munich* for
Munchen, or a thousand other similar equivalents. Custom is the
only thing in favour of *Cinchona*, but custom is not easily altered."

Thus it is admitted that the form *Chinchona* is
absolutely right in the abstract, and personally the
highest authority would prefer the correct spelling.
But it is considered that words are *means* not *ends*,
and that in nine cases out of ten custom and habit
are so strong, that it is impossible to correct an
error when it is once generally adopted.

Now, in the first place, this case is exceptional,

because the name of the *Chinchona* genus *is* an
end as well as a means. Unlike the vast majority
of the names of plants, which are merely given
as empty compliments, and only serve as tickets
or labels to distinguish them, the name *Chinchona*
was given for the purpose of commemorating a very
important event in the history of man, and of immortalising the beneficent act of the Countess Ana.
Moreover, the form of spelling in common use
entirely frustrates this purpose, for *Cinchon* is a
word meaning a broad girdle or policeman's belt,
and *Cinchona* is absurd, and without meaning.
Then again the word *Cinchona* has never been
generally adopted. It was protested against from
the very first, by the highest authorities. So that,
while nine out of ten cases of bad spelling are
persisted in, the name derived from the *Countess
of Chinchon* ought, for the above and other reasons,
to be spelt correctly, and to be the tenth and more
auspicious case. There is one instance of the name
of a plant having been corrected, and of the correct
spelling having been generally adopted ; the claim of
which to such good fortune was much less strong than
that of the Countess's namesake. I allude to the
genus *Buffonia*, named after Buffon. Linnæus

originally spelt it *Bufonia*, but the error was subsequently corrected, and the correct spelling is now generally adopted.* But this name did not commemorate any important event connected with the genus, it is merely an end, not a means; and the omission of one *f* but slightly altered the word. While the name of *Chinchona* does commemorate a great event, it is an end as well as a means, and the omission of the first *h* so mangles and mutilates the meaning, as to change it from a noble title, famous in history, to a policeman's belt. Such is the difference between *Chinchon* and *cinchon*. Surely if *Buffonia* is to be spelt right, *a fortiori* the *Chinchona* genus should be also.

The difficulty with regard to indexes can readily be got over by making a cross reference.

Another eminent advocate of the mutilated form is the well-known scientific traveller, and the distinguished author of the *Histoire Naturelle des Quinquinas*, in which valuable work he unfortunately adopted the wrong spelling. At the meeting of the International Horticultural Exhibition, in the sum-

---

* Lindley's *Vegetable Kingdom*, p. 497.

L

mer of 1866, Dr Weddell made the following remarks :—

"With regard to the spelling of the generic name of the bark tree, Linnæus, and almost every modern botanist, write it *Cinchona*, while Mr Howard, following in this respect Ruiz and Pavon, and other old Spanish botanists, would have it *Chinchona*. Which of these modes of spelling ought we to adopt? The last, undoubtedly, if it can be proved that Linnæus committed an error in dropping the first *h* of the *Countess of Chinchon's* name ; but this cannot even be surmised ; he did so for the sake of euphony, just in the same way as he wrote *Jussiæa* instead of *Jussieua*, and so on. Now, the question of priority being undoubted, no further reason than this ought to be required for establishing the preference in favour of Linnæus. It may, however, be further argued, that the spelling advocated by Mr Howard does not, in reality, attain the end he has sought for better than the original one ; the Spanish particle *ch*, to be pronounced as in the English word *church*, not being so pronounced in any other language than English. In Italian, indeed, the sound is given by *c* alone. Another disadvantage derived from the proposed change, would be that of creating a precedent to which, in numerous other cases, it would be absolutely impossible to adhere. When, for instance, two different genera have been dedicated to the same botanist, and their names have a common derivation, such as *Fontanesia* and *Desfontainea*, which, according to the proposed new rule, ought both to become *Desfontainesia*. And after all, would the Countess of Chinchon's rights be in any way impaired by her name passing to posterity under a more agreeable form ? "

Dr Weddell thus concedes that *Chinchona* is undoubtedly the correct spelling, and that it should be adopted, if the erroneous spelling used by

Linnæus was not intentional. Now, as Dr Seemann has pointed out, the fact that Linnæus, in his different editions, used two spellings, *Cinhona* and *Cinchona*, proves beyond any possibility of doubt that the great botanist was not wedded to any special form of error, and furnishes strong presumptive evidence that his mistake was not intentional, and that the change in the spelling arose from a desire for accuracy.

The suggestion that Linnæus committed the error for the sake of euphony is therefore quite inadmissible, even if it were possible to conceive that he would think for a moment of improving the euphony of a word belonging to the most majestic and euphonious language in Europe. The example relied upon by Dr Weddell is quite inapplicable. The alteration of the *terminations* of unmanageable French names such as *Jussieu* in order to make Latin endings possible, cannot be quoted as analogous to the omission of an important consonant in the *first syllable* of a Spanish word. And, even if the consonant was in the last syllable, there never can be any necessity, on the ground of euphony, for altering a Spanish word to give it a Latin termination.

Dr Weddell supports the wrong spelling on the

ground that the question of priority is in favour of Linnæus; but it has been shown that Linnæus spelt it in two ways, both wrong; and *Cinhona* has just as good a claim to preference, on this ground, as *Cinchona.* Both being wrong, and the claim of each being equal, while they cannot both be adopted, the propriety of adopting the correct spelling becomes evident.

Dr. Weddell then enters upon the question of pronunciation, which is really quite irrelevant. If only the English and Spanish pronounce the word correctly, let other people pronounce it in any way they please, but in the name of common sense do not spell the word wrong because you do not choose to pronounce it right.

The supposed danger of making a precedent is groundless for two reasons. In the first place, this is altogether an exceptional case; and in the second, it could not form a precedent. A broad distinction must be drawn between names which have been spelt wrong through inadvertence, such as *Bufonia* for *Buffonia, Cinchona* for *Chinchona, Plumeria* for *Plumieria;* and words the last syllables of which have been altered for the sake of euphony, as *Jussiœa* instead of *Jussieua.* But *Chinchona* cannot be a precedent, because it stands on distinct grounds from the others. While other names are merely means, this name was given to serve an end. In quoting the existence of two genera dedicated to the same botanist, Dr Weddell surely cannot approve the practice of calling more than one genus after the same man, and distinguishing them by adopting various erroneous ways of mutilating his name!

In conclusion, I feel very strongly, and I know that my feeling is shared by many persons who take an interest in the subject, that the Countess Ana's right is not only impaired by converting her name into that for a policeman's belt—which is very far from being a more agreeable form; but that in so doing the intention of Linnæus to do her honour is entirely frustrated, and her name is treated with disrespect, and mutilated by those who are bound to venerate her memory, and at least to offer that slight tribute of reverence which would be shown by refraining from spelling her title wrong.

I now come to the reasons for spelling the word correctly. The various pleas for the wrong way having been disposed of, this Memoir will fitly conclude with a statement of the case in favour of that noble lady whose memory deserves to be had in honour by this and all future generations.

1. All authorities agree that *Chinchona* is correct, and that consequently *Cinhona*, *Cinchona*, and all other forms are wrong. This is one point in its favour.

2. Most botanical names are means, not ends; and their uses as means once established, botanists persist in spelling them wrong, when an error is once generally adopted. But the error now under discussion has never been generally adopted, and the name for the *Chinchona* genus, as has already been pointed out, is an end, and a very important one, as well as a means. It was not given merely as a distinguishing label, and as an idle compliment, but was selected for a particular reason closely connected with the history of the genus. It is impossible to conceive a more appropriate name for the plants yielding. that inestimable febrifuge, the use of which is essential to the welfare of mankind, than that of the noble lady who first made its virtues generally known. Others, besides botanists, are interested in preserving that revered name from mutilation; and if the continuance of established errors is

to be the general rule in botany, most assuredly
no case ever had a stronger claim to being treated
as an exception than this one.

3. The only real ground upon which the misspelling can possibly be defended is that of convenience. If every one spells the word wrong, it
may be inconvenient and confusing to spell it right.
But this is very far from being the case. If an
inquirer wishes for information respecting the
quinine-yielding trees of New Granada, he must
necessarily refer to Mutis and Zea, who spell the
word *Chinchona.* If he would study the valuable
species yielding the red bark, he must turn to the
reports of Spruce, where the word is spelt *Chinchona.*
If he would know about the crown barks of Loxa
or the grey barks of Huanuco, his authorities must
be Ruiz and Pavon, who spell the word correctly.
If he desires to learn the particulars of the exceed-
ingly important results attained by cultivating the
plants in India, still the word is *Chinchona* in
the cultivators' reports. So it is in official
correspondence, in all the Blue Books presented
to Parliament, and in the narratives of those who
have recently explored the South American
Chinchona forests. It is true that some indis-

pensable authorities, such as Bonpland, Poeppig,
Weddell, and Karsten spell the name wrong, but
they are in a decided minority; and a continuance
of the misspelling is likely to be inconvenient and
confusing to the increasing number of persons
who are practically interested in the *Chinchona*
genus.

To sum up, the correct spelling should be
universally adopted because it is right, because
the mutilation of the name entirely frustrates the
laudable object with which it was given, and
because the form *Chinchona* is most convenient,
while the wrong spelling is inconvenient and
confusing, as well as unsightly and incorrect.

I therefore plead for justice to the memory of
my honoured client in the name of that great
botanist who desired to make it immortal, and
who would have been the first to correct his
own error had it been pointed out to him before
his death; in the name of those zealous Spanish
explorers of the *Chinchona* forests who earnestly
pleaded for the correct spelling during their lives;
in the name of millions who should know to whom
they are indebted for the priceless febrifuge which
saved their lives, and who cannot recognise her

in the corrupt and mangled form which the
advocates of error give to her name. I plead
for the correct spelling, as a tribute of respect
to a great historical family, now passed away;
as a right which may justly be claimed by the
people of *Chinchon;* and as the only way by
which the memory may be preserved of her who
made known to the world the inestimable value
of quina bark, who was thus a benefactor to
mankind, but whose monument has been destroyed,
whose place knows her descendants no more,
the illustrious and beautiful lady, ANA DE OSORIO,
4TH COUNTESS OF CHINCHON.

APPENDIX.

APPENDIX.

A COMPLETE LIST OF ALL THE SPECIES WHICH HAVE BEEN NAMED AFTER THE LADY ANA DE OSORIO, COUNTESS OF CHINCHON.

1. *Chinchona acanelada* (*Pav.*)
2. ,, *acuminata* (*Poir.*) Cascarilla acuminata
3. ,, *acutifolia* (*R. P.*) ,, acutifolia
4. ,, *affinis* (*Wedd.*)
5. ,, *Afro India.* ( ) Danais fragrans
6. ,, *amygdalifolia* (*Wedd.*)
7. ,, *angustifolia* (*Swartz*) Exostemma angustifolia
8. ,, *asperifolia* (*Wedd.*)
9. ,, *Australis* (*Wedd.*)
10. ,, *Azaharito* (*Pavon*) Cascarilla magnifolia.
11. ,, *Barbacoensis* (*Karsten*)
12. ,, *Bergeniana* (*Mart.*) Remijia Bergeniana
13. ,, *Boliviana* (*Wedd.*)
14. ,, *Bogotensis* (*Karsten*)
15. ,, *brachycarpa* (*Swartz*) Exostemma brachycarpa
16. ,, *Brasiliensis* ( ) Machaonia Brasiliensis
17. ,, *caduciflora* (*H. B.*) Cascarilla magnifolia
18. ,, *Calisaya* (*Wedd.*)
    ,, ,, var. *Vera*
    ,, ,, ,, *Josephiana*
    ,, ,, ,, *Ledgeriana*
19. ,, *Caravayensis* (*Wedd.*)
20. ,, *Caribæa* (*Jacq.*) Exostemma Caribæa

21.	*Chinchona*	*Caroliniana (Poir.)* Pinckneya pubens
22.	„	*Cava (Pavon)* Cascarilla Pavonii
23.	„	*Chahuarguera (Pavon)*
24.	„	*China (Lopez)* Cosmibuena obtusifolia
25.	„	*Chlororrhiza (Bry)* Danais rotundifolia
26.	„	*Chomeliana (Wedd.)*
27.	„	*coccinea (Pav.)*
28.	„	*Condaminea (H. B.)*
29.	„	*conglomerata (Pav.)*
30.	„	*cordifolia (Mutis)*
31.	„	*coriacea (Poir.)* Exostemma coriacea
32.	„	*corymbifera (Forst)* „ corymbifera
33.	„	*crassifolia (Pavon)* Cascarilla calyptrata
34.	„	*corymbosa (Karsten)*
35.	„	*crispa (Tafalla)*
36.	„	*Cujabensis (Manso)* Remijia Cujabensis
37.	„	*decurrentifolia (Pavon)*
38.	„	*dichotoma (R. P.)* Ladenbergia dichotoma
39.	„	*dissimiflora (Mutis)* Exostemma dissimiflora
40.	„	*erythrantha (Pavon)*
41.	„	*excelsa (Roxb.)* Hymenodictyon excelsum
42.	„	*ferruginea (St Hil.)* Remijia ferruginea
43.	„	*firmula (Mart.)* „ firmula
44.	„	*flaccida (Willd.)* Hymenodictyon flaccidum
45.	„	*floribunda (Swtz.)* Exostemma floribunda
46.	„	*fusca (Ruiz)* Lasionema rosea
47.	„	*glandulifera (R. P.)*
48.	„	*globiflora (Pav.)* Nauclea Chinchonea
49.	„	*grandiflora (R. P.)* Cosmibuena obtusifolia
50.	„	*grandifolia (Poir.)* Cascarilla magnifolia
51.	„	*gratissima (Wall.)* Luculia gratissima
52.	„	*Hänkeana (Bartl.)* Palicourea Hänkeana
53.	„	*Henleana (Karsten)*
54.	„	*heterocarpa (Karsten)* Cascarilla nitida

55. *Chinchona heterophylla (Pavon)*
56. „ *hexandra (Dietr.)* Casearilla hexandra
57. „ *hirsuta (R. P.)*
58. „ *Humboldtiana (Lamb.)*
59. „ „ *(R. et Sch.)* Lasionema Humboldtiana
60. „ *Jamaicensis (Wright)* Exostemma Caribæum
61. „ *Kattucamba (Retz)* Uncaria acida
62. „ *laccifera (Tafalla)* Condaminea tinctorea
63. „ *Lambertiana (Mart.)* Cascarilla Lambertiana
64. „ *lanceolata (Pavon)*
65. „ *lancifolia (Mutis)*
66. „ *lineata (Vahl)* Exostemma lineatum
67. „ *longiflora (Lamb.)* „ longiflorum
68. „ „ *(Mutis)* Cosmibuena obtusifolia
69. „ *Luciana (Vitm.)* Exostemma floribundum
70. „ *lucumæfolia (Pavon)*
71. „ *lutea (Pavon)*
72. „ *lutescens (Ruiz)* Cascarilla magnifolia
73. „ *macrocalyx (Pavon)*
74. „ *macrocarpa (Vahl)* Cascarilla macrocarpa
75. „ *macrocnemia (Mart.)* Remijia macrocnemia
76. „ *macrophylla (Karsten)*
77. „ *magniflora (Pavon)* Cascarilla macrocarpa
78. „ *magnifolia (Pavon)* „ magnifolia
79. „ *micrantha (R. P.)*
80. „ *microphylla (Pavon)*
81. „ *Montana (Radd.)* Exostemma floribundum
82. „ *Moritziana (Karsten)* Ladenbergia Moritziana
83. „ *Mutisii (Wedd.)*
84. „ *Muzonensis (Goudot)* Cascarilla Muzonensis
85. „ *nitida (R. P.)*
86. „ „ *(Benth.)* Cascarilla nitida
87. „ *oblongifolia (Lamb.)* Cascarilla Riveroana
88. „ „ *(Mutis)* „ magnifolia

89.	*Chinchona*	*obovata* (*Pavon*)
90.	„	„ (*Willd.*) Hymenodictyon obovatum
91.	„	*obtusifolia* (*Pavon*)
92.	„	*officinalis* (*Linn.*)
		„ ˙*var. Condaminea* (*Markham*)
		„ „ *Bonplandiana* (*Markham*)
		„ „ *crispa* (*Markham*) *
93.	„	*ovalifolia* (*H. B.*) Lasionema Humboldtiana
94.	„	„ (*Mutis*) Cascarilla macrocarpa
95.	„	*ovalis* (*Cav.*)
96.	„	*ovata* (*R. P.*)
97.	„	*Pahudiana* (*Howard*)
98.	„	*Palalba* (*Pavon*)
99.	„	*Palton* (*Pavon*)
100.	„	*parabolica* (*Pavon*)
101.	„	*parviflora* (*Mutis*)
102.	„	*Pavonii* (*Don.*) Cascarilla Pavonii
103.	„	*pedunculata* (*Karsten*)
104.	„	*Peruviana* (*Poir.*) Exostemma Peruviana
105.	„	„ (*Howard*)
106.	„	*Philipica* (*Cav.*) Exostemma Philipica
107.	„	*Pitayensis*
108.	„	*prismatostylis* (*Karsten*) Cascarilla
109.	„	*pubescens* (*Vahl*)
110.	„	*purpurascens* (*Weddell*)
111.	„	*purpurea* (*Pavon*) ˙
112.	„	*Quina* (*Lop.*) Cosmibuena obtusifolia
113.	„	*racemosa* (*Schr.*) Exostemma Caribæum

˙* *C. officinalis* is the original species named by Linnæus. Humboldt and Bonpland altered it to C. Condaminea, but Dr Hooker has restored the old name. The above varieties are cultivated in India and Ceylon. The names were given by me (*Memorandum* 18, *Feb.* 1863, *Parliamentary Blue Book*, p. 254, Part I.) with Dr Hooker's full approval; but simply as a matter of convenience.

114. *Chinchona* *Remijiana* (*St Hil.*) Remijia Hilarii
115.   ,,   ,,   (*Spr.*)   ,,   ,,
116.   ,,   *Riedeliana* (*Ca.*) Cascarilla Riedeliana
117.   ,,   *Roraimæ* (*Benth.*) Cascarilla Roraimæ
118.   ,,   *rosea* (*R. P.*) Lasionema rosea
119.   ,,   *rugosa* (*Pavon*)
120.   ,,   *Sanctæ Luciæ* (*David*) Exostemma floribunda
121.   ,,   *scrobiculata* (*Weddell*)
122.   ,,   *spinosa* (*Vavass*) Catesbœa Vavasorii
123.   ,,   *Sterocarpa* (*Lamb.*) Cascarilla Sterocarpa
124.   ,,   *stupea* (*Pavon*)
125.   ,,   *subcordata* (*Pavon*)
126.   ,,   *suberosa* (*Pavon*)
127.   ,,   *succirubra* (*Pavon*)
128.   ,,   *Tarontaron* (*Pavon*)
129.   ,,   *thyrsifolia* (*Willd.*) Hymenodictyon thyrsifolium
130.   ,,   *Timorensis* (*Span.*) Hymenodictyon Timorense
131.   ,,   *triflora* (*Wright*) Exostemma triflora
132.   ,,   *Trianæ* (*Karsten*)
133.   ,,   *Tucuyensis* (*Karsten*)
134.   ,,   *umbellulifera* (*Pavon*)
135.   ,,   *undata* (*Karsten*)
136.   ,,   *undulata* (*Tafalla*)
137.   ,,   *Uritusinga* (*Pavon*)
138.   ,,   *Vellozii* (*St Hil.*) Remijia Vellozii
139.   ,,   *villosa* (*Pavon*)
140.   ,,   *violacea* (*Pavon*)
141.   ,,   *viridiflora* (*Pavon*)
142.   ,,   *Tovarensis* (*Karsten*)

The *Chinchona* genus has given its name to
the family of which it is a member—the *Chinchonaceæ*, including coffees, and several genera,

N

such as Gardenias, Hindsias, Ixoras, *Chinchonas*, Catesbœas, the fragrance and beauty of whose flowers are unsurpassed in the vegetable kingdom.

The family also includes ipecacuanha. The family of *Chinchonaceæ* in their turn give their name to Lindley's *Chinchonal* alliance, which consists of *Chinchonaceæ*, Vaccineæ or cranberries, Columelliaceæ, Caprifoliaceæ or honeysuckles, and Galliaceæ or madders.

Of the febrifuge alkaloids extracted from the *Chinchona* bark, three are named after the *Countess of Chinchon*, namely:—

1. *Chinchonine*
2. *Chinchonidine*
3. *Chinchonicine*

and five from the native name for the bark: *quina*—namely:—

1. Quinine
2. Quinidine
3. Quinicine
4. Quinamine
5. Quinoidine

ANOTHER ADHERENT OF THE CORRECT SPELLING.

Report on Class XLIV. *of the Paris Universal Exhibition.*
(*Chemical Products.*) By C. W. Quin, F.C.S.

" It will be noticed that throughout the above article we have adopted Mr J. E. Howard's method of spelling the word *Chin-chona* and its derivatives. The word being derived from the patronymic of the Countess of Chinchon, the first patient who experienced the curative effect of Peruvian bark, it should certainly be spelt *Chinchona.*"

The Laboratory of May 25*th, and June* 1*st,* 1867.

PRINTED BY BALLANTYNE AND COMPANY
EDINBURGH AND LONDON

www.ingramcontent.com/pod-product-compliance
Lightning Source LLC
Chambersburg PA
CBHW032110010726
47493CB00008B/2524